Wings
of the Dawn

Tracie J. Peterson

Heartsong Presents

With thanks to Steve DeWolf who took me flying in his Stearman biplane one beautiful Dallas morning and who inadvertently taught me that often in life you only get to answer yes or no.

A note from the Author:
I love to hear from my readers! You may correspond with me by writing:

Tracie J. Peterson
Author Relations
P.O. Box 719
Uhrichsville, OH 44683

ISBN 1-57748-066-X

WINGS OF THE DAWN

Cover illustration by Gary Maria.

PRINTED IN THE U.S.A.

one

Everything remained unchanged. And yet nothing was the same.

Cheryl Fairchild put down her small suitcase and stared at the familiar walls of her father's house. Nestled against a mountainous backdrop on one side and the Denver skyline on another, this place had been their home off and on for the last ten years. But now Ben Fairchild was dead. Dead by his own hand. Cheryl still found it impossible to believe. Any minute now he would surely call out from his office wanting to know what outlandish way Cheryl had spent money that day. Any minute now. . .

But of course, Ben Fairchild didn't call out, and Cheryl grimaced at the stuffiness of the closed-up house. For nearly four months she'd been in either the hospital or the private convalescent center, and during that time, the housekeeper had only come on Saturdays in order to keep the dust at bay. It was evident that she never bothered to air the place or check the thermostat, Cheryl thought, sweltering in the heat of the July afternoon.

Switching on the central air, Cheryl listened for the familiar hum of cool air blowing through the vents. When it came, it was like an old friend. Familiar. Comforting. Consistent. Forgetting the suitcase, Cheryl wandered aimlessly through the house, touching first one thing and then another. Almost as if she had to force some memory from each article before she could move on to the next.

Daddy and I bought this vase in France, she remembered,

idly fingering the elegant Lalique crystal. *We found it at that wonderful shop near our hotel. Daddy said, "If your mother were alive, she'd pick this one." And so we did.*

A bevy of other objects received just as much attention until Cheryl had walked completely through the spacious first floor and found herself once again standing beside her suitcase. Her side ached a little. A constant reminder of the bullet that had been surgically removed some four months earlier. The scar was still there, while the one that had marred her forehead had been expensively removed with plastic surgery. For the first time in weeks, Cheryl let herself think about the shooting. . .and Stratton.

No, she reminded herself, *his name is Grant Burks*. He wasn't Stratton McFarland as he had told her when they first met. Nor was he really Stratton McFarland when he had proposed marriage and she had accepted. And he wasn't Stratton McFarland when he had deceived her into believing that it didn't matter what you did with your life—so long as it made you happy.

She picked up the suitcase and made her way upstairs to her bedroom. Here, the heat was worse, and Cheryl thought only of a cool shower and lightweight clothes. She stripped down, leaving her designer jeans and flashy pullover on the carpet, and stepped into her private bathroom. The reflection of her hollow-eyed expression stunned Cheryl momentarily. Months before, she wouldn't have been caught dead looking so unkempt and dowdy. Her blond, curly hair looked more askew than normal, and her collarbone and ribs stuck out in an anorexic way that was most unflattering. But she didn't care anymore. There was no reason to care, because there was no one left to care for.

She showered and dressed in an oversized T-shirt that had once belonged to her father. Long ago she had claimed it for her own and used it as her favorite nightgown. Now it was just one more reminder of her father, and for the present time, she needed it to help her through the loneliness that threatened to consume her soul.

With a sigh, she sat down on her bed and noticed for the first time that a stack of mail lay there awaiting her inspection. There was something else there as well. A black book, an album of sorts, had been neatly placed beneath the mail, and it was this that drew Cheryl's attention. Cautiously, almost reverently, she opened the book and found cut-out headlines representing the last six months or so of her life.

Mary must have done this, she thought. The housekeeper was fond of cutting out any public announcements of her employer and saving them for his consideration. Now, perhaps, she felt Cheryl should take over that job as well.

It seemed odd to hold the pages of one's life in a single book. The headline announcing her father's suicide opened the chapter and Cheryl forced herself to read the details aloud.

"Ben Fairchild, cofounder of O&F Aviation Corporation, was found shot to death in his downtown office today. Police are ruling the death a suicide. Fairchild was the focus of an intense Drug Enforcement Administration investigation, and it is rumored that charges were soon to be leveled in connection with a national drug smuggling ring."

Cheryl fell silent. There was no way they would ever convince her that her father had been corrupt. Ben Fairchild had been a paragon of virtue. He had given liberally to charities, had received multiple community action awards, and had never failed to make certain Cheryl had everything she needed. He was a good father and citizen, she assured herself. He couldn't possibly do the things they accused him of.

She turned the pages and saw articles that laid out the foundation for the DEA's suspicions towards her father. Those suspicions were only heightened when it was discovered that Ben had transferred everything he'd owned into Cheryl's name some two years prior to the investigation. Cheryl had known nothing about this. The house, the cars, stock, money markets, bank accounts, even the businesses her father had built were all officially the property of Cheryl Fairchild. It was almost too much to consider.

Toward the end of the book, Cheryl came across an article that told of her own misfortune. "DEA Drug Bust Claims Victims," the headline read. Cheryl held her breath for a moment, then let it out slowly. This was where her life had ended. This was where the love of her life had been killed and the baby she'd hoped to give him had miscarried.

"DEA Officer Curtiss O'Sullivan. . ." She couldn't read past the name. Curt had been an intricate part of her life. His father had been her father's partner in O&F Aviation. They had wooed the country with aerial barnstorming shows and biplane exhibitions. Her father had maintained the business dealings, while Curt and his father had performed the actual flying feats. Cheryl and Curt's sister, CJ, had become fast friends, while Cheryl had lost her heart completely to CJ's gangly adolescent brother.

They had grown up as one family, or very nearly. The O'Sullivans and Fairchilds were quite inseparable. They worked together, vacationed together, raised children together. *And now*, Cheryl thought, *they are dead together*.

Cheryl's mother had passed away many years earlier from cancer, and CJ and Curt's parents had died in an airplane crash. It was that same crash that had left a sixteen-year-old CJ horribly injured. Cheryl had been engaged to Curt at the time, but he'd rapidly changed after the death of his parents, and now Cheryl knew why. The night of the plane crash, Curt's father had telephoned him to say that he'd discovered cocaine on board one of the planes, and Curt immediately picked up the banner of what would become his private crusade. Their breakup had hurt, but not nearly as badly as knowing that Curt was responsible for the death of Grant, and in some ways, her baby as well.

Cheryl put her hands to her flat stomach, and a shudder ran through her from head to toe. She'd known it was wrong to give in to Grant's desires, but she'd been so confident that nothing bad could come of it. CJ had tried to warn her—to convince her that God had a better way in mind—but Cheryl wanted nothing of religion and rules. Grant showed her a side of life that said rules were unimportant so long as you had plenty of money. With plenty of money, you could buy new rules or make up your own as you went along. And Cheryl found that it worked. At least for a while.

She tried hard not to think of the child who would never be born. She tried hard not to think of the emptiness inside her when she knew the baby was gone for good. She slammed the book shut and dropped it as though it had grown red hot. She couldn't let herself think about the past anymore.

"Ha," she said sarcastically, "as if I could ever forget."

She shuffled downstairs, the T-shirt bobbing at her knees, her bare feet sinking deep into the plush, supple carpet. She had no idea what she was going to do with herself for the rest of the day, but even this seemed taken from her control at the sound of the doorbell.

She pushed back damp curls and stared at the door for several moments. *Who could it possibly be?* The bell rang again.

"Who. . .who is it?" Cheryl called out nervously.

"It's CJ, Cheryl. Come on and open up."

Cheryl slowly opened the door and stared at the petite red-haired woman. "I'm not up for visitors, CJ," she said flatly.

"I was worried about you," CJ said, seeming to ignore Cheryl's tone. "I thought you were going to let me bring you home."

"I never agreed to that." Cheryl noted the hurt expression on CJ's face but continued. "I told you before, I can't deal with you just now."

"I don't understand."

"It isn't that hard," Cheryl replied. "Your brother ruined my life."

"That's not really true, Cheryl, and you know it," CJ countered.

Cheryl's anger erupted without warning. "What would you know of the truth? You've lived in a shell most of your life. First with your picture-perfect family, then hidden away from the world in the misery you felt after the death of your parents." CJ paled, but Cheryl was unrelenting. "You have your husband and your wonderful life, so please don't feel like you need to show pity on me. I don't want it, nor do I need it."

"I wasn't offering you pity, Cheryl. I thought we were friends."

"*Were* friends," Cheryl repeated. "We were friends."

"But not now, is that it?" CJ's eyes filled with tears. "You're going to throw away a lifetime of friendship because of what has happened?"

"You say that as though nothing of great importance has transpired. As though you put a scratch on my car or a hole in my favorite sweater." Cheryl looked hard at CJ for a moment and tried to feel something other than rage. It was impossible, however. She couldn't stop the flow of words that came.

"I've lost everything that mattered to me. My father is dead. Stratton—" she paused and shook her head, "Grant is dead. My baby is dead. Do you suppose I care very much that your feelings are hurt because I don't want your friendship? Do you suppose I care at all whether I ever see you again, knowing that just seeing your face reminds me of the man who murdered my loved ones?"

CJ was now openly weeping. "Don't be like this. Curt was only doing his job." She struggled to keep control of her voice. "Curt didn't want to kill him, but Grant pulled a gun and started shooting. It was Grant's bullets that struck you, did you forget that? He was trying to kill my brother."

Cheryl refused to be moved by the display of sorrow or by CJ's words. "Curt didn't have to start the whole thing."

"You mean let the murder of my parents go unpunished?" CJ questioned, sobering a bit. "That's it, isn't it? You'd rather my parents' murder be swept under the rug so that business could go on as usual. Ben could have kept his little drug-ring secrets, and Grant or Stratton or whatever other name he used could go on deceiving you."

"If it meant bringing back my loved ones, then yes," Cheryl answered coldly. "Now I'd like for you to leave. I told you before that I haven't the energy to deal with this."

"But I care about you," CJ said, wiping her eyes. "I know that you're just using your anger to camouflage the pain. I want you to know that you aren't alone. I still care and so does God."

"Don't give me that religious song and dance you're so fond of. God didn't care enough to keep my baby from dying or protect my father from your brother's slanderous accusations. And God certainly didn't care about Grant."

"But you're wrong," CJ replied. "God cared for each of them. Is it His fault that Grant and Ben wanted nothing to do with Him?

"Get out." Cheryl's voice was deadly calm. "Get out and take your God with you. I don't have to listen to this now or ever."

CJ turned to leave but hesitated for just a moment. "Cheryl, I want you to know that when you are ready for a friend, I'm here for you. I won't stop caring about you just because you say mean things, so if you're using that to push me away, it won't work."

A strange sensation coursed through Cheryl. Looking into CJ's eyes, Cheryl could read the sincerity and love her friend held for her. But just as quickly as she recognized this truth, Cheryl pushed it away. To see the truth of CJ's concern meant that her own beliefs of needing to endure injustice and suffering alone were invalid.

"There's nothing more to be said, CJ, unless it's to make clear to that brother of yours that if he ever sets foot on my property, I'll personally even the score."

CJ's eyes widened in shock at the threat, but it mattered little to Cheryl. She watched CJ go and slammed the door hard. Closed doors were all she would ever give CJ from this moment on. It was a promise she made herself, and for reasons beyond her understanding, it gave her a moment of peace.

two

"But you don't understand," Erik Connors told his sister and her husband. "Cheryl Fairchild is, in my opinion, suicidal. No doctor in his right mind should have released her, even if her physical wounds were healed."

"Erik, it isn't your concern," his sister Christy offered. "If the doctors okayed her release, then you can't interfere with that. Besides, Cheryl allowed herself to be mixed up with Grant Burks, and now she's paying the piper. Don't forget, she was the 'other woman' in our little sister's short married life."

Erik nodded, knowing full well that their sister had suffered greatly because of Grant's infidelity. Candy had barely been old enough to marry when she'd fallen in love with Grant Burks, and in spite of both Christy and Erik's misgivings, she had married him and found herself almost immediately pregnant.

"But Christy, Cheryl didn't know he was married to Candy. She had no way of knowing that he had a wife and baby on the way. To my way of thinking, she was just as duped as Candy was."

Curt O'Sullivan nodded. "I think that's true in many senses." He exchanged a brief apologetic smile with his wife. "I don't think that it makes what happened justified or right, however. Cheryl has always lived life in the fast lane. Her father taught her that, and he lived the example right up until the end. It was one of the biggest reasons I had to cut off my engagement with Cheryl."

"Good thing, too," Christy said with a loving smile.

"Well, despite her fast-lane approach to life," Erik said seriously, "she deserves forgiveness for her mistakes. God isn't going to hold a grudge against her, and I don't see where we have the right to, if God Himself doesn't plan to."

"She has to want to be forgiven," Curt interrupted. "She has to seek repentance, recognizing that she was wrong in the first place. So far, I don't see that Cheryl feels she has anything to confess."

"But given all that she's just come through, she's got to be doing a great deal of soul-searching."

"Erik, that is a matter of opinion, and not only that," Curt added, "but what makes you think Cheryl's brand of soul-searching includes wanting to hear about God from a complete stranger?"

"Who better? I don't hold anything against her, so it isn't like you or CJ going to see her. Cheryl has no past with me through which she might just feel even more ashamed, and she knows me from the hospital."

"I can't help but think she's going to feel a very strong past with you," Christy interjected, "even if you don't want her to feel that way. Once you explain the connection and she realizes that you're Candy's brother, she won't want anything else to do with you."

"Christy's probably right," Curt replied.

From upstairs came the cry of a baby. "Well, that will be Sarah expecting to be fed," said Christy, getting to her feet. Sarah, the baby Candy had given birth to shortly before succumbing to a brain tumor, had come into Christy's life much in the same way her husband Curt had. Most unexpected, yet most welcomed. Erik knew his sister held a deep abiding love for both of them, and he'd never seen her happier.

"Does she pack it away like her daddy?" Erik asked, noting Curt's second helping of barbecued ribs.

"She's worse," Curt said, grinning. "At least I don't cry at the top of my lungs."

Christy laughed. "I'd say it's debatable as to who makes more noise. It just depends on the day."

Erik smiled, while Curt ignored this comment and dug into his food. With Christy gone, Erik felt like he could get more personal about Cheryl.

"Look, Curt, I know Cheryl Fairchild is a sore subject, but I'm hoping that at least you will try to understand my thinking in this. I feel led to go to her. I've prayed all of this through, and count it a 'holy mission' or whatever else you want to call it, but I feel somehow responsible to extend Christian charity and love to that woman."

"Cheryl will never take it," Curt replied. "Mark my words. She'll have you thrown from the house faster than you can say, 'Jesus saves.'"

"But she talked to me in the hospital. I used to have to draw blood from her on my morning collection rounds. I sympathized with her situation and commented on her recovery, and she always seemed to respond."

"Throwing a pitcher of water at you can hardly be deemed a positive response."

Erik laughed. "Yes, but it was only that one time. After that, I made sure things were kept out of reach when I came into the room. Besides, she threw things at everybody."

Curt leaned forward and put down his fork. "Look, Erik, I know you have a big heart, and I'm certainly not trying to tell you to disregard something God has directed you to do—if, indeed, God has directed you to minister to Cheryl. I'm simply saying that once Cheryl finds out how you are related to Grant, she'll have nothing more to do with you."

"But like I said, Curt," Erik began again, "she was duped by Grant, and she has to know that we don't hate her for it. She must be feeling fifteen kinds of fool for her involvement with him. Just imagine all the rhetoric and lies he must have told her to get her to surrender to his charms. Even you said that Cheryl wasn't the kind of person to go from man to man and that she was most likely pure when she came to Grant."

"But what if she doesn't feel like a fool? You are presuming that Cheryl sees the errors of her ways, and I'm telling you that the Cheryl Fairchild I know may well think herself completely in the right. She probably believes that she and Grant were the victims in this mess and that the rest of us are unfeeling liars who planted evidence and strung up the wrong man."

"But you said that once everything sunk in—"

"I remember what I said." Curt sighed. "Once she *allows* everything to sink in, she'll see the truth of the matter for herself. And when she does that, she's going to feel worse yet. Seeing how stupid you were and being smacked in the face with your mistaken judgment and actions is not something that anyone handles well. Cheryl will be especially hard to deal with in this area, mainly because as far as she's concerned, she's never been wrong about anything."

"So you think I should stay away from her because she'll never believe me, is that it?" Erik questioned honestly.

"That and the fact that I also don't want my investigation messed up because you interfered in a matter you should have stayed completely out of."

Erik looked at his brother-in-law and tried to figure out how to present his case in such a way that Curt might better respect his plan. Ever since he'd learned of Cheryl

Fairchild's plight and misguided involvement with Grant Burks, Erik had felt a strange concern for her. The more he learned about her, the more he found himself wanting to help.

"She's gone through so much." Erik tried another approach. "The surgeries, losing the baby, recovering from severe intestinal damage—all of it took its toll. She was lucky to only have to endure a temporary colostomy instead of a permanent one, 'cause I can tell you from firsthand knowledge, the initial opinions on her condition weren't that great. The surgeon thought that *if* she lived through the operation, she'd be permanently disabled in one way or another."

"I know all of this, Erik. And now that her physical injuries are healed and she's nearly the same old Cheryl in body that she was before, she's more messed up inside than a simple visit and 'Hey, I'm praying for you, kid,' is going to fix."

Erik felt suddenly put off by Curt's attitude. "I'm not suggesting that I'm going to drop in and preform a miracle. You make it sound like I think that I alone can put her on the road to spiritual healing. Like I expect to walk on water. It isn't that at all."

"Then what is it?" Curt asked, eyeing him seriously.

"I'm the only one who's offering to help," he answered matter-of-factly. "I don't see anyone else going the distance with her."

"My sister tried," Curt said softly. "That's why I know Cheryl won't take kindly to any kind of spiritual lecturing or pat, formula responses. I know this lady well enough to say this," he paused as if trying to word what he would say in a precise and exact manner. "If Cheryl is determined to kill herself, you won't stop her. She doesn't do things by halves, and she doesn't care what anyone else thinks about her. The only person in the world she really cared about was her father, and he's dead. Next in line was probably Grant Burks, and he's dead, too. So you see, I have very serious doubts that anything you say or do will be the slightest bit positive."

"I have to try, Curt," Erik said, getting up from the table.

"Try what?" Christy asked as she returned to the room, balancing five-month-old Sarah against her shoulder.

"Your brother believes he has a mission to witness to Cheryl Fairchild, and even though I've tried to dissuade him, Erik feels he has to reach her."

Christy frowned. "To what purpose, Erik?"

"To the purpose of helping her find salvation," Erik replied. "You may not think her reachable, but I believe there is a great need inside that woman. I don't intend for her to slip away without at least offering her the means to find her way back to God."

He left the room, feeling for all the world as though a huge weight had fallen upon his shoulders. For all his time working in the hospital and on the mission field during his summer vacations, Erik had never before had a case present itself in such a way that it demanded his complete attention. But Cheryl Fairchild had stirred up a consciousness inside him that he couldn't ignore. She was needy and hurting, but then, so were many others he'd seen in his twenty-five years. What exactly made Cheryl different was a mystery to Erik.

Sliding into his aged Chevy pickup, Erik turned the key and listened to the engine roar to life. She might not be much to look at, but even when the windchill registered twenty below zero, this truck would start as smooth and easy as if it were a summer's day. And with a four-speed transmission and a four-bolt main for an engine, Erik could compete with the newest four-wheelers in exploring the mountainous back roads.

"They just don't understand," he said as though the truck were a living companion. "If I don't at least try to reach her, I'll never be able to live with myself."

three

Cheryl stared at the flamboyant clothes hanging in her huge walk-in closet. These were the clothes of a very confident woman. These were the clothes of a woman who knew what she wanted and wasn't afraid to go after it. She pulled a red, sequined number from the hanger and studied it for a moment. The halter-style bodice left little to the imagination either on the hanger or off. Tossing it to the middle of her bedroom floor, Cheryl reached for another. This time a silky black sheath slipped from the satin-covered hanger. She had been wearing this dress the first time she'd met Grant.

Grant. It was still so hard to get used to calling him that, and yet Cheryl knew that it was his real name. Still, it had been the name Stratton that she'd whispered in tender "I love you's," and Stratton was the name signed to all her love letters and cards.

The black sheath joined the red gown on the floor, and after those first few moments of deep consideration, Cheryl rapidly eliminated nearly every article of clothing from her closet. She finished by tossing aside the maid of honor dress she'd worn at CJ's wedding. Standing back, she stared at the massive pile.

What should she do with it all? She couldn't very well set it on fire, although that was her first thought. These clothes represented a large portion of her adult life. So much time and care had gone into shopping for just the right outfit, for just the right affair. She'd rather enjoyed the attention it had brought her, and while she knew people thought her overly extravagant and flashy, Cheryl thought it very important to dress her role.

But what's my role now? she wondered, still staring at the mess she'd made.

She picked up the telephone and dialed directory assistance.

"Yes, I need the number for one of those charity organization who handle second-hand clothes." Pause. "Yes, Goodwill, Salvation Army, any one of those is fine." She listened as the number was given, then hung up the phone and redialed.

"This is Cheryl Fairchild. I have a large number of next-to-new clothing items that I would like to donate to your organization." She listened as a woman rattled on about the type of clothing they were interested in before interrupting. "Look, can someone just come get these things?"

The woman objected and began to give a list of reasons for why Cheryl should bring them in herself. "Ma'am, I just got out of the hospital, and I'm unable to bring myself to your address. I have clothing here worth hundreds of thousands of dollars. Do you want them or not?"

This seemed to bring the woman to life, and with little more said, Cheryl gave her the address and promised to be waiting that afternoon for their man to arrive.

With that taken care of, Cheryl went to her father's closet and pulled on one of his white oxford shirts. It had been freshly laundered and pressed and still hung inside the dry-cleaner's plastic wrapping, but nevertheless, it made her feel closer to her dad. She accompanied the shirt with an old pair of baggy black sweats and padded down the stairs barefoot to see what else the day might offer her.

Passing the mirror in the hall, Cheryl hardly recognized her own reflection. She looked like a bag lady with her unkempt hair and mismatched clothes. But she didn't care. She never intended to step foot outside the house again, so what did it matter if she looked a fright?

The morning passed by painfully slowly, and Cheryl found that the only way to keep her mind occupied was to keep her body busy. She made one trip after the other up and down the stairs to deliver her clothes to a growing pile in the living room. The tenderness of her left side made her think about taking a break, but she was too fearful of what might happen if she gave in and rested. *No sense in having a pity party in the middle of the day*, she reasoned. *Better to save that for the night.*

She had made the last trip downstairs and had just deposited the last of the clothes into a pile nearly as tall as herself, when the doorbell signaled the arrival of the delivery man. At least, that was who she'd presumed would greet her from the other side of the door. Instead, she found the familiar face of a man who'd worked in the hospital where she'd convalesced.

"Hi," Erik Connors said. Smiling rather sheepishly he added, "How are you feeling?"

Cheryl was taken aback by the handsome young man. He was tanned from the summer sun, and his jogging shorts and T-shirt made it clear that his lifestyle lent itself to a great deal of physical activity.

"I'm fine. What are you doing here? Is this a part of that home-care service I told them to forget about?"

Erik shook his head. "No. I didn't come here on hospital business."

"What then?"

"I was kind of. . ." he paused and actually grew red in the face. "I was worried about you."

Cheryl found his words disconcerting. "I don't understand. Why would you be worried about me?"

"Well, it's just that—" Erik paused, looked at the ground, and seemed to struggle to continue. "Look, could I just come in for a few minutes? I want to talk to you."

"I hardly think that would be appropriate," Cheryl answered in a no-nonsense manner that she hoped would put him off.

"Appropriate or not," Erik countered, seeming to regain his self-assurance, "I need to talk to you."

"Why?"

"Because I care about you."

Cheryl looked him for a moment and read nothing but genuine sincerity in his expression. "You have no reason to concern yourself with me. I'm no longer a patient, and the doctors have given me a complete release from medical care."

"Look, I know all about that, but this is different."

"How is it different?" she asked suspiciously.

"This is personal. You don't understand, but there are things which connect us to each other's lives and I, well—"

"Look, if you're thinking of asking me out, forget it," Cheryl said, backing up in order to close the front door in his face.

"No!" Erik exclaimed and put his hand out to halt her progress. "I didn't come for a date. I came because I know you're hurting. I know that you were deceived, and I know that you believe no one in this world cares for you."

Cheryl pulled the door back very slowly. She stared at the handsome face, noting laugh lines at the corners of his blue eyes. "And just how do you know all this? Surely the blood you drew from me didn't reveal this information."

"No, it didn't," Erik admitted. "The truth is, Cheryl, I'm Erik Connors."

Cheryl shook her head. "Should that mean something to me?"

"My sister Christy is married to Curt O'Sullivan. My little sister Candy was married to Grant Burks."

Cheryl felt the blood drain from her face. Her breathing came in tight, strained gasps. "Get out! Get off my property, and leave me alone!"

"I want to help you," Erik insisted. "Look, I know you must feel pretty bad after all you've gone through, but I want you to know that I don't hold you responsible for Grant's actions. You were as much a victim of his deception as my sister was."

Cheryl gave a strained little laugh. "Victim? I was no victim. I loved the man, and I can't help it if. . .if. . ." She strained for air and began wheezing and gasping. "Can't. . . breathe."

Cheryl felt herself in complete panic. Putting her hand to her throat, she tried desperately to calm her rapid breathing. It was as if air was going in, but nothing was coming back out.

Erik took hold of her. "Breath in through your nose and out through your mouth. You're hyperventilating."

Cheryl shook her head and pushed him away. She wasn't going to listen to this man. He was her enemy. He could offer her nothing but pain and misery. Still gasping, she felt the room begin to spin, and her vision tunneled down with blackness creeping in from every side.

Let me die, she thought, feeling her knees begin to buckle.

Erik half carried, half dragged her to the couch. He forced her to sit down, then pushed her head forward until her face was on her knees. "Breathe in through your nose and out through your mouth. Come on, Cheryl. Long, deep breaths. Force yourself to listen."

Cheryl found herself responding almost against her will. It was as if Erik were breathing for her. In. . .out. . .in. . .out. Over and over she forced the calming breaths deeper into her lungs until the blackness faded and the dizziness passed. She felt helpless and weak, and her side ached terribly from the position in which she was bent.

"Better?" he asked most compassionately.

She nodded, afraid to speak. Gently, he eased her back against the couch and eyed her with a look of consuming attention. "I'm going to get you a glass of water and a cool cloth. You stay right here, and I mean right here. Understand?"

She nodded again, but remained silent. She watched him as he glanced first one way and then the other, searching for some sign of the kitchen or bathroom. She wanted to be angry with him for his interference, but for some reason, she felt sorry for him, and this emotion seemed to calm her further.

He was back in a matter of minutes with the promised items. Cheryl obediently drank sips of cool water and allowed Erik to place the cold cloth on the back of her neck.

"I'm really sorry," he apologized. "I never meant to cause you further harm. Curt and Christy warned me that you might not take too well to my company, and I guess I pushed too hard."

Cheryl took another sip of water and securely put up her defenses. "You have no reason to be here. I'm not your concern."

"I know that, but in another way, I know just as well that you are my concern."

"That makes no sense whatsoever, Mr. Connors."

"I know, but if you would just give me a chance to explain."

"Hello!" called a voice from the still-open front door.

Cheryl sat up abruptly, fearful of who this latest visitor might be. "Yes?" she called out apprehensively.

"I'm here to pick up some clothes," a man called back.

Erik eyed the multicolored pile in the middle of the living room. "Doing all your dry cleaning at once?" he asked with a smile.

Cheryl ignored the humor. "More like early fall cleaning or late spring cleaning," she replied, then raised her voice. "In here!"

The man, dressed in brown work clothes, entered from the hall foyer and dropped his mouth open in surprise at the huge mound of clothes. "Wow! I've never seen that many—" He paused and looked at Cheryl as if trying to rethink his thoughts. "I mean, you sure you want to get rid of all these, lady?"

"Absolutely sure," Cheryl replied and, ignoring Erik's concerned expression, got to her feet. "If you want to be helpful, Mr. Connors, why don't you assist this gentleman in removing these things from my house?"

Erik looked as though he wanted to say something important, but instead he nodded and turned to the workman. "Well, what say we get at it. I wouldn't be at all surprised to find some lost civilization buried beneath that mess."

The man grinned good-naturedly, and Cheryl found the entire matter uncomfortable. She didn't want to smile or laugh. She didn't want to feel good for even a single minute. Feeling good meant that there was a reason to go on living, and she didn't want there to be a reason to go on. She wanted to end her life, and the sooner she arranged for all her affairs to be properly in order, the better.

Leaving the men to make short work of her affairs, Cheryl took herself into the family room and switched on the television. Two children danced and giggled while their mother snapped pictures of them and advertised the quality of her particular film. Cheryl watched the little girls, their faces beaming smiles at the camera, their eyes lit up in anticipation of the moment.

"I might have had a daughter," she murmured to the empty room.

The commercial passed and another came on advertising, "What to do when those morning aches and pains got you down." Cheryl flipped the switch off and went to the window. Staring out over the backyard, she noticed the sorry state of things for the first time. Weeds grew around the fountain and fishpond. This had been the centerpiece of her father's landscaping, and Cheryl couldn't let it be consumed by neglect.

But if you're dead, what will it matter? a voice seemed to question inside her head.

"Cheryl?" Erik called out.

Cheryl swallowed back an angry retort and returned to the living room. "Why are you still here?"

"I didn't want to just leave without saying good-bye," Erik said with a smile.

"Good-bye, then," she replied and turned to go.

"No, wait," Erik called after her.

"I have nothing more to say, Mr. Connors. Please show yourself out."

She refused to look back, and only after she was out of sight, did Cheryl pause to listen for the sounds that would signal Erik's departure. His footsteps sounded on the marble in the foyer, and then the closing of the door echoed in the stillness around her.

Good, she thought. *Let that be the end of it.*

four

"So how's the investigation going?" Erik asked.

Curt looked up from his newspaper and shrugged. "Okay, I guess. There's a great deal that remains a mystery. Maybe Cheryl will be able to shed some light on it for me."

"Cheryl? You mean *you* plan to interview her?" Erik grew hopeful. This would be the perfect way to see Cheryl again. He'd actually be there for a reason.

". . .Later today," Curt finished and resumed reading his paper.

"Wait. What did you say?"

Curt gave up on the paper and folded it back together. "I said that Cheryl may have information that will be key to our investigation, and I'm going to her house later today."

"Can I come along?" Erik asked.

"No way. This is DEA business."

"But Cheryl's in a fragile state of mind. I told you what happened the other day and how she hyperventilated. You know from your own sister that she blames you for Grant's death and that she never wants to see you again."

Curt frowned. "It doesn't matter. I have to go. I can read Cheryl like a book, and no one else has that advantage. And although it sounds rather cruel, I can also use her dislike of me to get the answers I want. People under stress often blurt out things they'd never consider speaking of in calmer times."

"That is rather cruel," Erik agreed. "Especially when it's a friend."

Curt sighed and pushed out of the overstuffed chair. "Look, drugs are dirty business and people get hurt. You know from what Christy has told you that even when she was suspected of aiding that same drug ring, I couldn't just drop her off the list of suspects. Even though I'd fallen in love with her and was certain she had no knowledge of what was going on, I still had to investigate her, and I still have to investigate Cheryl."

"But it's so soon," Erik protested. "Don't you care about her recovery?"

"It's been four months," Curt replied. "She was left alone as much as possible during the last few months because I stuck my neck out for her. And because I'm one of the owners of O&F Aviation and have worked from the beginning to keep the feds in the middle of the organization, they were a little more sympathetic to my suggestion. That's not going to carry her the rest of her life, however. She's going to have to answer some very detailed questions. After all, our records show that Ben Fairchild transferred all of his business interests to Cheryl some time ago. That makes her as much a part of this as it does me or CJ or even Grant. Ignorance isn't going to carry a great deal of weight in a court of law, and I for one hate to see O&F property remain under seizure for much longer."

Erik realized his mistake in suggesting that Curt might not care about Cheryl. "Hey, I'm sorry. I should have known." He quickly moved the conversation forward. "So you're going there this afternoon?"

Curt glanced at his watch and headed over to his desk to pick up some papers. "Yeah, in fact, I need to put in about two hours over at the office before I see Cheryl, so if you don't mind, I'm going to leave you to lock up."

"That's okay. I'll just leave now."

"You want me to drop you somewhere? Home?" Curt asked.

Erik glanced down at his jogging clothes and shook his head. "No, I need to run. I should never have weakened and stopped by. It's just that I saw your car here and wanted to know about Cheryl."

"No problem."

They parted company, and Erik considered his brother-in-law's words all the way back to his apartment. He might not be able to accompany Curt in a professional way, but what if he just happened to be at Cheryl's house when Curt showed up? A plan began to formulate in his mind. Curt had said that he'd be at the office for a couple of hours. That would give Erik time enough to clean up and get over to Cheryl's before Curt arrived. He picked up speed with each passing thought. *She might not want my company*, he thought, *but once she finds out that Curt is on the way, she's going to need the extra support.* He smiled to himself and, without even feeling winded, jogged up his apartment stairs. His plan would work.

⋙

Erik rang the doorbell and waited for Cheryl to appear. When she did, he had to hide his surprise at her appearance. She didn't look like she'd had a bath all week, and her hair was matted and lifeless. Her face registered only mild disgust at seeing him, and Erik played upon her surprise.

"Hey, how are you doing?" he said enthusiastically. "I thought I'd stop by and see if you felt like some company."

"I told you to stay away from me," Cheryl responded. "What do I have to do—get a restraining order?"

Erik laughed and tried to keep matters lighthearted. "I'm not stalking you, if that's what you think. I just wanted to offer you a day of sunshine." He waved behind him and added, "And a pleasant companion."

Cheryl's expression remained the same. "I'm not interested in seeing you or anyone else for any reason at all." She began to close door.

"Then you'd better rethink your plans because Curt O'Sullivan is on his way over here right now. I thought you could use some moral support."

Cheryl threw open the door. The color had drained from her face and her blue eyes were wide in fear. "Curt is coming here?"

Erik nodded. "I asked him if I could come along, and he refused. Said it was all business and I should keep out of it. But you know already how persistent I am. I just didn't want you to have to face the DEA's questions alone."

Cheryl's gaze darted back and forth, and she craned her neck forward to see if Curt might already be there before she yanked on Erik's shirt to drag him inside the house. "I can't deal with him," she said flatly. "Will you take me away from here?"

"Take you away to where?" Erik asked, so stunned by this sudden change of events that he didn't know what to do.

"Anywhere! It doesn't matter." She glanced down at her clothes—cut-off jeans and a baggy black T-shirt. "I need shoes. Wait here."

Erik stared after her without quite knowing what to do. As she ran upstairs, his mind raced with the implications of what he'd just done. He'd blown Curt's surprise visit, and he'd inadvertently interfered with a DEA investigation. It wasn't something he relished admitting to.

Cheryl returned quickly, socks and blue hiking shoes in hand. "Hurry, he'll be here any minute."

"There's no way of knowing that—" Erik began.

Cheryl interrupted him, flailing the socks for emphasis. "Then you don't know Curt like I do. I feel it in my bones. Come on."

"But Cheryl, he's with the DEA. You can't just walk away from them. You and your father have a great deal to answer for."

Cheryl gave him a stunned look of disbelief. "You think I had something to do with this?"

Erik felt in heart that she couldn't possibly have known about her father's dirty deeds. He smiled. "No, I don't believe you did. But," he tried to give her what he hoped was his most sympathetic expression, "it doesn't matter what I think. The DEA has their own idea about things and—"

"Will you stop talking? Are you going to take me away from here, or am I going to have to take myself?"

Erik felt that in some way he owed her. "All right." He motioned to her shoes and socks. "Get those on and we'll go."

"I'll put them on *as* we go," she insisted.

She started to push him forward, but Erik was still torn. "Look, Curt understands your situation. He kept the feds pretty much at bay while you were sick these last months."

Cheryl laughed, and the sound was hollow and bitter. "If you call plaguing me day after day about my relationship to Grant Burks and whether my father had any hidden assets at bay, then yes, I suppose they were most congenial."

"But they have to know the truth."

Cheryl's expression grew angry, almost hateful. "The truth has never mattered as much as making themselves look good and my father look bad. Now come on."

With Cheryl pulling him to the truck, there was little he could do but flat-out refuse. But he didn't want to refuse her. She was reaching out to him, even if it was for all the wrong reasons, and he wanted to help calm her and make her realize that he cared greatly for her well-being.

He opened the pickup door, noting that she didn't think twice about scrambling up into the cab. A lot of women frowned upon realizing that they were going to be expected to ride in what he called "Ole Blue." But not Cheryl Fairchild. At that moment, Erik realized that he could have been driving a garbage truck and her response would have been the same.

He jumped into the driver's seat and fired up the engine, cautiously keeping an eye out for Curt's arrival. If they managed to make their escape before Curt pulled into the drive, Erik knew he'd have a great deal to explain later. Throwing the truck into gear and praying at the same time that God would somehow intervene and keep his actions from causing too much trouble, Erik pulled out onto the street.

"Where to?"

"It doesn't matter, so long as you get me away from here," Cheryl said, forcing her foot into the shoe. She glanced up to give the neighborhood a quick once-over before resuming her task. "Can't this thing go any faster?"

"This is a residential district," Erik replied, pushing the speed as much as he dared. "I wouldn't want to break the law anymore than I already have."

"What do you mean?"

"I mean that I'm sure to be breaking multiple laws by helping you escape DEA questioning." He pulled up to a stop sign and turned to catch her doubtful expression.

"I hadn't thought of it that way," she answered softly. "I'm sorry. I never meant for this to happen. I shouldn't have asked you to take me away."

"No, I suppose you shouldn't have." Erik grinned. "But I'm glad you did."

"You are? Why?"

"Because now maybe you'll believe that I'm really on your side and that I care about you and what you've been through."

Cheryl nodded but turned away to look out her window. Erik smiled to himself and set the truck in motion. *Just don't let me mess this up, God*, he prayed. *I only want Cheryl to see that someone cares enough about her to be there for her. I only want to help her.*

⁂

Cheryl barely noticed the passing scenery. She saw places in Denver that she'd never before ventured into and probably never would again. And before long, Erik had wound through the city and was headed up into the mountains via a small, gravel back road.

He's a strange man, she thought, still not knowing quite what to make of him. He just waltzed into her life and with no more than a few well-placed words had somehow assigned himself her guardian angel. In this case, however, she was grateful. The last person in the world she wanted to have to deal with was Curt O'Sullivan. Just thinking about him made her boil. She balled her hands into tight fists and silently wished she could plant each one squarely into his face.

It seemed far easier to hate Curt than to deal with her loss. So long as she focused on the anger she felt for him and the revenge that she one day hoped to have against him, Cheryl could make her way through the day and night with some semblance of order. Curt was the reason she was alone. Curt was the one who should pay.

"Look, now that you're my captive audience, so to

speak, I'm hoping to say a few things."

Cheryl glanced up and noted the determined set of Erik's jaw. Even though his face almost always seemed to be on the verge of an impish grin, this time there was something more serious about his expression.

"Well, say what you want. I suppose I owe you for getting me out of there," Cheryl replied.

"I was serious when I told you that I cared. My family has suffered a great deal in this, too. There's a baby without her parents because of this."

"A baby?" This was the first Cheryl had heard of it.

"You remember the baby Grant had you watch for him at the mall? The day of the shooting?"

Cheryl remembered quite well. She wrapped her arms around her waist and hugged them close. "Yes."

"That little girl is my niece Sarah. She was my sister's baby. My sister and Grant's."

Cheryl swallowed hard, remembering that Grant had told her they were watching the baby for his sister-in-law. Curiosity got the better of her. "Why was she there?"

"Sarah? Grant was using her as a trading piece. Christy, my older sister," he paused and smiled. "I forgot that you know Christy."

"She was making my wedding dress," Cheryl replied off-handedly.

"Yeah, well, Christy was supposed to adopt Sarah. Just before she died, Candy begged Christy to keep Sarah from Grant. She knew that he would only use the baby to get whatever he wanted, and Candy had given her life for that child."

"What do you mean she'd given her life?"

"Candy had an inoperable brain tumor. The doctors could have given her chemo or other treatment, but she refused because she was pregnant. Candy wanted nothing to interfere in the life of that unborn baby, and she was willing to take the chance that she'd not give birth in time to receive treatment for the cancer. I thought at first she was crazy, but the more I thought about it, the more I understood, and I think you can too. A child is a sacred gift from God."

"Then He seems to be quite contradictory in His giving," she muttered.

"I know you lost a baby, Cheryl," Erik said, lowering his voice almost reverently. "And while I'm a man and can't possibly know what it is to carry life inside me, I grieve for you and your loss."

Cheryl's eyes filled with tears. No one had ever said such a kind thing to her before. CJ had said that God had a purpose in everything, and the doctor had assured her that she could have other children, as though she'd lost her choice of a new automobile, instead of the life of her baby. But Erik said he grieved with her. Erik offered to bear the burden alongside of her, instead of relegating her to a hidden corner where unwed mothers should bury their faces in shame.

"So you don't think God killed my baby because I was evil?" Cheryl said sarcastically.

"No, I don't think God killed your baby. I think Grant did. Frankly, I think it's possible he knew exactly what he was doing."

"How dare you!" Cheryl exclaimed.

"I dare because Curt told me the details of the shoot-out. You threw yourself between Grant and Curt. Grant had plenty of time to recognize that you were there. Maybe too much. After all, if you think about it, he had to redirect his line of fire in order to hit you in the abdomen. He'd already grazed Curt's arm, so shooting you in the head could have been explained away as accidental. Your head was in the line of fire from which Grant was already shooting. But if you're honest about it, you'll realize the truth in what I'm saying. Grant had to deliberately lower his aim to hit you low enough to end his baby's life."

"Stop it!" Cheryl cried out, putting her hands to her ears. What he said made startling, ugly sense, and she couldn't deal with the thought that Grant had purposely tried to kill not only her, but their baby as well.

Erik pulled into a short dirt turnaround beside a rushing stream. He turned off the engine and rolled down his window. Then shifting to better look at Cheryl, he suggested she do the same thing in order to enjoy the fresh air. Reluctantly, she did as she was told.

"Please listen to what I want to say. Then, I promise if it absolutely makes no sense, not even one thread of sense, I'll drop it. But I won't stop caring about you, and I won't just go away as easily as you put everyone else off."

Cheryl shook her head. "Why not? No one else needs to be told twice. Why are you such a hard case? Are you some kind of nut or what?"

Erik laughed. "I suppose in a way. When I was a teenager, there was a popular saying in our youth group. 'I'm a fool for Jesus, whose fool are you?' I thought it made a lot of sense. You sold out to one thing or another in life. What mattered was which thing you chose. But I suppose the biggest reason I'm determined to stick this out with you is that I feel a sense of responsibility for you."

"Why? I'm nothing to you. You never knew I existed before the shooting."

"I knew someone existed."

"I don't understand."

"I knew Grant was deceiving someone, if not a great

many someones. I was praying for you even back then."

Cheryl looked away and noticed the stream for the first time. With the window down, it was easy to be caught up in the sounds of the water as it traveled over the rocks. "CJ was always praying for me," she murmured.

"I know. Curt told me how worried she was about you. See, Cheryl, you can try to shut out the rest of the world and even believe that you've accomplished just that, but somehow things are far more complicated than we give them credit for. Did you know that not only is CJ praying for you, but her husband prays for you as well? Then there's my sister Christy and Curt."

"Please don't mention his name," Cheryl said, turning to face Erik's compassionate gaze. "I don't want to talk about him. I can't talk about him."

"Sooner or later you're going to have to talk about him. And not only *about* him, but *to* him. He's not the kind to stand back, and he won't leave you alone forever. Just because we've thwarted his efforts this time is no indication we can do it again."

"But if Curt hadn't started all of this. . ." She fell silent and bit her lower lip.

"Curt didn't start this, and the sooner you accept that, the better you'll feel. But that's not what I wanted to say to you just now. I want you to know that God really does love you, Cheryl. He does listen to the prayers of His children, and with so many people praying for you just now, He's getting an earful."

She said nothing, and he continued. "God tells us in His Word that He will never forsake us, and Cheryl, I believe He will be faithful to that promise. Even when we are disobedient, I don't believe God stands idle. I believe God uses the Holy Spirit to prick our consciences and teach us that some things are unacceptable, even when they seem our only way out.

"You gave in to Grant's demands," he paused, picking his words carefully. "You gave yourself to Grant in a way that went against what God had in mind, but it doesn't mean you can't be forgiven. You trusted a man who was evil and whose actions proved it, but still you can be forgiven. You lived a lifestyle that had no room for God, but He never left—never stopped loving you. He still stands with open arms, waiting for you to see that planning out things your own way will only lead to this kind of misery."

"So now all of this is my fault?" Cheryl questioned, struggling with the strange sensation Erik's words caused within her heart.

"You are partially to blame, aren't you? Weren't you the one who went willingly into the relationship with Grant? Weren't you the one who gave in to Grant, even when you didn't want to—even when you knew it was wrong?"

"CJ's told me all this mumbo-jumbo before. I didn't buy into it then, and I don't see a reason to buy into it now. God can't possibly care about me now, anyway. I'm the scum of the earth, as you so eloquently pointed out."

"I said nothing of the kind! I only tried to say that we all make mistakes, and God is willing to forgive us—when we are willing to repent."

"I can't live in a little box," Cheryl said and then easily recognized that this was exactly how she was living. She shrugged and noted the time. "Don't you think Curt will have given up on me by now?"

"Possibly. Do you want me to take you back?"

"Yes, please."

They stopped for fast food on the way back to her house, and Erik insisted that she eat it under his supervision. He drove around Denver until she had managed to finish the cheeseburger and fries. She hadn't believed herself hungry, but by the time she was halfway through, she felt quite ravenous.

Erik pulled into her drive, but when he reached for the keys, Cheryl put her hand over his and stopped him. "Don't."

"I thought maybe—"

"Look," she began, "I appreciate what you did today, but I don't want you to worry about me or see me as some pet project of yours. I'm beyond saving, and you needn't waste your time with me."

"I don't think I'm wasting my time," he replied.

"It doesn't matter what you think," Cheryl said, rather stiffly. "I'm not interested in buying what you're selling, and I think it would be best if you don't come back here again."

She got out of the truck without waiting for his reaction or response. A part of her wished he would come after her and convince her that she was wrong, but an even bigger part wanted to run as fast as she could. Away from Erik Connors and his kindness. Away from Erik Connors and his God.

five

One day blended into another, and for Cheryl, very little happened to mark the passing weeks. She spent a great deal of time in her father's study and bedroom. Sometimes she'd lie down on his bed and try to imagine happier days when she'd been a little girl and her mother had still been alive. The memories, dimmed from the years, were the only thing that gave her the slightest comfort. They were probably the only reason Cheryl hadn't taken the drastic way out and ended her life.

She looked around her father's room, feeling so alone and sad that she had to do something in order to rally herself. Opening first one drawer and then another, Cheryl pulled out clean clothes, undershirts, sweats, and pullovers for working outside. She rubbed the material with her hand, thinking all the while of Ben Fairchild and what his absence meant to her. Her entire world had turned around him, and now he was gone.

She pulled out the drawer containing his socks and other personal articles and dumped the contents on his bed. Suddenly she noticed that a lockbox had been taped to the outside of the back of the drawer. She peered into the hole where the dresser drawer had resided and found a hollowed out indentation that matched the size of the box. Her father had intended to hide this box from any casual search, and suddenly it seemed quite valuable to Cheryl.

Pulling the strips of duct tape off, she held the box at eye level. It was a simple gray metal box, no bigger than five by eight, with a small locking mechanism to secure the lid. She tried to open it and found it was locked tight.

Setting the lockbox aside, Cheryl searched through her father's things for a key and came up empty-handed. *There must be some way to get that box open,* she thought and finally retrieved a screwdriver and pried the lock apart. When the lid flew back, Cheryl could only gasp in surprise. On top, a stack of thousand-dollar bills greeted her like a flag of warning. Carefully she picked up the money and counted out fifty thousand dollars. She shuddered. *What was Daddy ever thinking to keep this much money in the house?*

She set the money aside and pulled out two computer diskettes, a set of keys, and several pieces of paper which had been folded neatly together and placed on the bottom. She opened the papers, wondering even as she did if this was the information Curt wanted so desperately. Was this the final shred of incriminating evidence that would forever brand her father a drug trafficker?

The first page read like a Chinese encrypted menu. There were symbols and numbers, dollar signs and totals, all given in neat, orderly columns. The second paper gave a list of street addresses, usually followed by some brief, abbreviated set of directions.

"Third row, second shelf, back. Black/telephone-direct. See J.M.," she read from one line. *What in the world did it mean?*

The more she read, the worse the feeling she got in the pit of her stomach. Surely this information proved more than she was ready to accept. Her father was obviously involved in something he wanted to keep hidden. After all, he'd gone to all this trouble to put the box into hiding behind the dresser drawer.

With a sensation that someone might be watching her, yet knowing it was impossible, Cheryl thrust the contents back inside the lockbox and resecured the lid. It was an awkward fit after her work with the screwdriver, but she forced it to close and tucked the box under her arm. She would have to hide it away. Hide it where no one could find it. Not Curt and his friends nor anyone else who might have need of what was inside.

She hurried to her room and looked around for a proper hiding place. She thought first of her closet where the striking emptiness was sure to draw immediate attention to any object left inside. That would never do. Next she thought of burying it in a box of personal items that she'd planned to give to Good Will. But that, too, seemed a likely place for someone to look. She sat down on the bed and rubbed her hands back and forth across the lid as she thought. *It would have to be somewhere where it wouldn't seem likely to be. But where?*

Then an idea hit her, and Cheryl jumped off the bed and ran to her private bathroom. Her combination shower/tub had a wonderful ledge that had been designed to hold her toiletry items, and for years one end of the tiling had been loose. Her father had put off having it repaired because he wanted to redo the bathroom in imported marble. Now it seemed that his negligence would go one step farther in preserving his reputation.

Cheryl stepped into the tub and pushed aside her shampoos and bath oils. She studied the situation for a moment, determined to make certain that whatever she did, she wouldn't draw attention to the ledge. She put the lockbox on the floor of the bathtub and played around with the loose corner of the tile. With a little work it loosened even more, and before long the white caulking came apart altogether and the tile was free. Underneath, Cheryl could see that the entire ledge was nothing more than a boxed frame with waterproof tiling. This suited her purpose exactly.

Unable to tell how far down the boxing frame went, Cheryl quickly retrieved one of her belts and tied it around the lockbox. It was a tight fit getting the box past the small opening, but once this was done, the box floated freely for several inches before settling with a hollow "thunk" against the bathtub base.

Cheryl reached her arm through the opening and realized she could easily touch the box, so she let the belt drop into the hole and quickly put the tile back in place.

Stepping away, she frowned. It was quite noticeable that the tile wasn't in the same order as the rest of the ledge. The white caulking was shattered, with pieces in the tub and intermingled with her bath articles. She sat down on the tub and considered the situation for a moment. Then a revelation struck her, and Cheryl swung her legs over the edge so quickly she put a stitch in her side.

Toothpaste! she thought. Years ago when she'd lived in an apartment in California, the landlord had patched holes in her wall with toothpaste. It blended right in with the spackling and looked as though there had never been a nail to mar the purity of the wall.

Pulling out her toothpaste, Cheryl breathed a sigh of relief to find that the contents were white, just like the caulking around the tiles. She pulled a nail file from one of the drawers and went to work. First she smoothed off the remainders of the old caulking, and then she liberally applied the toothpaste and worked it into the seams of the tile until it matched perfectly with the rest of the shelf.

Feeling rather proud of her ingenuity, Cheryl replaced her shampoos and bath oils on top of the tile and stepped back to survey her work. Except for the crumbs of caulking in the tub, there didn't appear to be anything out of order. Cheryl smiled, completely satisfied with the results. Her last order of business was to turn on the faucet and wash the caulking down the drain.

She'd just walked from the bedroom when the telephone rang. She seldom ever answered it, but from time to time it was one of her doctors or some other matter that refused to be put to rest and so she was in the habit of letting the answering machine pick up the call while she listened in.

"You've reached the Fairchild residence," her father's voice boomed on the machine. "Leave a message at the tone." That was it. A simple, no-nonsense message. The machine beeped, and Cheryl waited in anticipation for the message which might be left.

"Yes, Ms. Fairchild, this is Anthony Zirth with the Denver *Post*. I'm doing a feature to honor your father and to award him the posthumous honor of—"

Cheryl picked up the telephone. "Hello, Mr. Zirth? This is Cheryl Fairchild."

"Ah. . .Ms. Fairchild," he said in a hesitant voice, "I didn't think you were in."

"I screen my calls very carefully," she replied rather coolly.

"I can well understand. You must surely receive a great many calls. May I say, first of all, how sorry I was to hear of your father's death?"

"Thank you. That's kind of you to say."

"He was a great man, and we here at the *Post* have planned to name him our man of the year. I was hoping to interview you and get your perspective on what it was like to be the daughter of such a man."

"I'm sorry," Cheryl said, trying hard to soften her voice.

"I don't do interviews. I've been through too much of late."

"Of course, that's understandable." The man positively oozed sympathetic concern. "I can do the story without your insight, but of course, it would make it much better with some type of personal touch. Say a photograph or some other bit of information you'd like the world to know about him?"

Cheryl thought for a moment. Mary's scrapbooks came to mind. Not the most recent one with all the black details of their lives, but earlier ones. Albums with comments about the awards he'd been given and copies of programs from gatherings given in Ben Fairchild's honor.

"I might be able to provide some of those things," she finally answered.

"If you could, I want you to know it will make this story truly great."

"Well then, Mr. Zirth, I realize tomorrow is Saturday, but if you can come by then, I'll have a few things put together for you."

"Tomorrow would be just fine. Would one o'clock suit you?"

"Yes, that's good for me."

She hung up the phone feeling another bit of elation. Someone wanted to honor her father. Someone still thought of him as a good man and not an evil drug-ring master.

She went to her father's study and found the albums she wanted. Next, she pulled down a family photo album and took out a picture of her father. It was her favorite one. He looked young and dashing in his three-piece suit. The photo had been taken for his company literature, but Cheryl thought it captured his personality better than any family photo they'd ever posed for. His look was determined, intelligent, and driven, and all of those things were the things she loved most about her father. He had taught her to be self-sufficient and confident. He had taught her to stare adversity in the face and come out swinging.

"Oh, Daddy," she murmured and tears filled her eyes, "what a disappointment I must be to you now." She continued talking to the photograph as if her father might really be listening. "I tried to be strong about all of this, but I just can't. I can't be *that* strong. There's nothing left. You're gone. Grant's gone. I just can't go on without you. There's nothing left. Nothing worth living for."

She broke down and cried with great painful sobs that wracked her body. From deep inside came a stark, hard hurt that would not be released with the simple deluge of tears. She pushed away from the desk and the photograph and thrust her father's office chair across the room as best she could. Next she picked up the trash can and threw it too. Before long, nothing was safe. She threw books, bric-a-brac, awards, trophies. Nothing mattered. Nothing was sacred.

When her anger was spent and the rage calmed within her, Cheryl surveyed the mess she'd made. It would take some doing to clean it all up, but at least it would give her a sense of purpose. Picking up the trash can, she sighed. *At least this will keep me from thinking.*

six

Guilt hung over Erik like a shroud, and he knew that he had to come clean with Curt about his outing with Cheryl. The O'Sullivan family barbecue at his sister's house hardly seemed the appropriate time or place, but Erik hoped that the setting and the fact that CJ and her husband were present would keep Curt from going ballistic.

"You did what!" Curt yelled when Erik tried to explain having gone to Cheryl that day.

"Just listen for a minute, Curt," Erik said, trying to explain his actions. "I only went there to offer her moral support. I thought if I came in on my own, she'd see that I was on her side and that I only wanted to help."

Curt was seething, and Erik could tell by the flushed color of his face that this was no minor issue that would be passed over with a brief justification. By this time, everyone else had stopped to see what the matter was. Christy was just approaching the two when Curt spoke.

"Inside, now!" he told Erik between clenched teeth.

"Curt? What's wrong?" Christy asked, stopping short of touching his arm.

"Your brother and I need to talk. Please try to understand, and explain to CJ and Brad that we'll be back in a few minutes."

"Is something wrong?" she asked again.

"You could say that," Curt said and stormed off toward the house.

Erik shrugged and added, "It's all my fault. I'll explain

it later."

He followed Curt into the stately Victorian house and made his way to the one room he knew Curt would seek refuge in, his own private study. Coming through the door, Erik could easily see that Curt was trying to get his emotions under control. He paced in front of the window and glanced up at Erik when he entered the room, but he clenched his teeth together even tighter and turned to look out the window rather than speak.

Erik felt terrible. He knew it was no more than he deserved, but he hated the fact that Curt was angry at him, and he hated even more that he deserved that anger.

"Before you start in on me," Erik said, "I want you to know that I take full responsibility for my actions. I know I was wrong, Curt, and I'm asking you to forgive me. It won't happen again."

Curt's shoulders seemed to relax a bit, but without turning around he asked, "Why should I believe that? I asked you to stay out of it in the first place. You didn't respect that request, so why would you respect any other?"

"Because I don't want this coming between us." Erik sat down and put his head in his hands. "I didn't want to do what I did. I knew it would mess up your plans, and yet she was so needy and so. . .well. . .helpless."

Curt turned on this. "Cheryl has never been helpless."

Erik looked up and met his expression. "Then you don't know her as well as you think you do. She's very vulnerable and not at all the pillar of strength that you seem to believe her. A strong woman wouldn't have given in to Grant Burks. Christy didn't."

Curt frowned. "She very nearly did. Oh, not on his suggestions that she become his mistress or anything like that. But she very nearly kept his cocaine activities to herself in order to protect Sarah and to some extent, to protect me."

Erik laughed. "Christy isn't a good example of a strong person, either. I think we both know the charade she plays when she's worried someone is going to get too close."

Curt smiled tightly at this, but his face instantly sobered. "That was no reason to interfere."

"No, it wasn't. I have no justifiable reason. It wasn't life or death, except maybe in Cheryl's own mind. But it was a matter of earning her trust, and Curt, I wanted that trust very badly."

"Apparently so. It must have meant a great deal if you were willing to threaten our relationship."

"Has it?"

"Has it what?"

"Threatened our relationship?"

Curt sat down behind his desk and shook his head. "Of course not. But honestly, Erik, you can't go around putting yourself in the middle of DEA business. Cheryl might be able to put this whole thing to rest, but she can't relay that information to me if I can't get to her in person. I don't want to hurt her. I've always cared deeply about her, and a part of me will always love her like a sister." Curt blew out an exasperated breath. "I'm tied to her in more ways than one, and there is a great deal of excess baggage that we both need to rid ourselves of. Some of it has nothing to do with the DEA."

"Like you killing Grant?" Erik asked seriously.

"It wasn't my idea. I've searched my heart in this matter, and I didn't instigate the shooting. Grant did. Furthermore, I didn't want to kill him. I only wanted him brought to justice."

"I can't say that I'm not glad he's dead," Erik responded, easing back in the chair and crossing his arms against his chest. "I wish I could be sorry that he died, but I'm not."

"I didn't say I was sorry he was dead, either. I am sorry I had to be the one to pull the trigger."

"As I recall from the paper and Christy's story, there were plenty of other people shooting that day. In fact, when Grant was killed, you were busy rescuing Cheryl."

Curt nodded. "Yes, but as far as Cheryl is concerned, it might as well have just been me alone firing the gun."

Erik could well imagine that the sad-faced blond would hold that very opinion. "She feels like you took everything away from her. Your investigation caused her father to come under unbearable pressure, and your organized DEA rendezvous put an end to her happily-ever-after plans with Grant and her baby."

"You aren't telling me anything I haven't already gone over a million times in my own mind. The investigation started out as a need for revenge, but it turned around to be a search for justice and something that would bring about good. I just didn't want my parents to have died in vain."

"But Cheryl can't understand that. In honoring your parents, you dishonored hers. Leastwise her father. She wouldn't even let me speak your name."

Curt winced. "I'm way too personally involved for my own good. I've argued for my position with the DEA in this case because I knew things that would take years to teach someone else. I also knew Cheryl, or thought I knew Cheryl, and I felt that it would afford me an edge that no one else could have. I'd proven over and over that I could remove myself from the personal aspect, but maybe that's no longer possible."

"Are you saying that you're going to remove yourself from the case?"

"I don't know. Maybe." He sighed. "Even if I do, I have

to resolve this matter with Cheryl."

"I guess I understand that," Erik answered. He let the silence remain between them for a few minutes before adding. "I intend to tell Cheryl that I've come clean with you. I won't interfere again, but I want you to know that neither will I abandon Cheryl. I feel like I made real progress with her the other day, and I want to play on that and see where it can go from there."

"I don't think that's wise," Curt said flatly. "I think you should stay out of her life all together."

"I respect your opinion, Curt, but I'm not going to do that."

Curt slammed his hands down on the desk. "You are going to cause more problems, and I'm not going to sit back and let it happen."

"You have no right to tell me who I can befriend. Get real, Curt. You may be an officer of the law, deep into investigating this woman, but you aren't going to boss me around like one of your subordinates." Erik felt his own anger piqued for the first time that day. He had come to Curt in apologetic humility, but now he felt only wounded pride.

"I'm telling you, Erik, it's only going to hurt her more."

Erik got to his feet. "You don't know that. You want to pretend that you have some inside track to the woman just because six or seven years ago you shared marriage plans. Well, I'm telling you that you know nothing of the Cheryl Fairchild who exists today. She's hurt, vulnerable, and very, very angry. I'm not going to let her bear that alone while you and your buddies rip her apart in hopes of exposing the truth about her father."

He stormed out of the house, mindless of the fact that Curt called after him. He paid no attention to Christy's pleading that he come tell her what was going on and instead, jumped into Ole Blue and ripped out of the drive.

Erik drove aimlessly through town until he found himself suddenly turning down Cheryl's street. In his heart he might have known all along that it was to Cheryl he was driving, but in his mind he argued the futility of it. Nevertheless, he turned into the drive and shut off the engine before he could change his mind.

He rang the bell and waited, watching and wondering if she would open the door to him. He thrust his hands deep into his jean's pockets and tried to force himself to remain calm. Soon, the door handle rattled and turned, and Cheryl appeared with a look of expectation on her face.

"Erik," she said and her expression fell.

Erik found her notably changed, although still quite dowdy from the Cheryl Fairchild he'd heard so much about. She wore a simple cotton skirt which flowed down to her ankles in a pastel flower print and a plain white cotton top. She looked airy and summery and better than he'd seen her since she'd entered the hospital. Maybe, just maybe, she was finally recovering emotionally.

"You look great!" Erik exclaimed. "What's the occasion?"

"Look, Erik, I asked you not to come around anymore." She glanced past him to the drive as if anticipating someone.

"You gonna have company?"

She nodded stiffly. "Yes, and I'd rather you go."

"Who's coming?"

"What?" she questioned, obviously distracted.

"Cheryl?"

She looked back to him and frowned. "A man from the Denver *Post* is coming to pick up some information and photographs."

"What information?"

Cheryl glanced down, seeming embarrassed. "I got a call yesterday from a man who is doing a feature on my father. The *Post* is naming my father Denver's man of the year."

"Did you confirm that?"

Cheryl's head snapped up, and she appeared quite hurt. "Why? Don't you think my dad deserves such a title?"

"I just think something like that ought to be checked out before handing personal items over. Did he ask you for a statement?" Erik asked suspiciously.

"He wanted a full interview, but I told him no."

"And did he accept that for an answer?"

"Look, stop giving me the third degree. You aren't my brother or the law, so stop asking so many questions." She was clearly agitated, and Erik didn't want to further alarm her. In his mind a million possibilities were playing themselves out. Who was this stranger, and was he acting on the up and up with Cheryl?

"Well," Erik said, taking hold of her arm and leading her back into the house, "I refuse to leave until after he comes and I feel certain he intends no harm."

Cheryl stared up at him in stunned surprise. "What are you doing? Let me go!" She jerked away, and Erik shrugged.

"Have it your way, but I stay."

"Fine!" she declared and crossed her arms against her chest.

Erik grinned. "Glad you're seeing it my way. Now, how about I fix us some lunch? I was supposed to have barbecue with my family, but I had to leave rather abruptly."

"I'm not hungry," she answered flatly and went to the front window to lift the curtain just enough to look out.

"Too bad," Erik replied. "I'm fixing us something anyway. I'll just be in the kitchen if you need me."

She said nothing, so he went off on his search. Something about the entire matter set his teeth on edge, and he had just reached the kitchen when the doorbell sounded. Turning on his heel, he started to head back to the living room when Cheryl's screams rent the air and made his blood run cold.

seven

Erik ran the final steps to the foyer where a strange man held a small microphone in one hand and clicked away with a camera with his other. Cheryl held her hands up to her face, screaming with every click and whir of the 35 mm.

"I just want to interview you!" the man declared over and over. "What was your involvement with Grant Burks? Were you involved trafficking in drugs with your father and Mr. Burks?"

Erik pushed his way between Cheryl and the man and grabbed the camera.

"Hey, you can't do that!" the man exclaimed.

"Oh yeah? Watch me!" Erik pulled the back open and exposed the film, tearing it from the safety of the camera and throwing it to the floor. He handed the stunned man his camera, then reached out for the mike. "Give me that tape recorder."

"Look, I just want an interview. She owes the public an explanation."

"She doesn't owe anyone, anything!"

Cheryl was still screaming and crying, and Erik's only thought was to remove the man and shelter her from further humiliation. Taking hold of the man by his shirt collar, Erik dragged him to his car.

"Give me the tape," he demanded, and the man finally gave up his fight and handed it over.

"You can't keep the world from learning the truth," the man said as he got into his car. "Sooner or later, someone is going to get her to talk. I figured it might as well be me as to be someone else."

"Well, you figured wrong, all the way around. If you ever show up here again, I'll personally take care of the problem." He knew he was angry and figured that the rage was evident on his face. He hoped he looked imposing. Apparently he did, for the man quickly nodded and started the car.

Erik hurried back into the house to find Cheryl still crying. Her hands were still protecting her face from view, and his heart went out to her. Closing the door, he took her in his arms and held her close. Her first response was to fight him, but he soothed her with soft words and gentle strokes.

"I won't let them hurt you," he whispered over and over. "You're safe now. I'm here, and I won't go until you feel better."

She grew still in his arms and, sobbing, put her head upon his shoulder. "He didn't even care about my father," she said.

"I know." Erik led her to the sofa and helped her to sit.

Cheryl gripped his arm tightly, and he had no other choice but to sit closely beside her. "He said he wanted to give Daddy an award. How could he be so cruel as to use my father to get to me like that?"

"People can be cruel."

She sobbed into her hands, and Erik pulled her against him and held her until her tears were spent. While she cried, he asked God to give her peace. He prayed, too, that God would use the tenderness he felt for her to bring her a better understanding of Jesus Christ.

"Nobody believes that my father was a good man. CJ thinks he killed her parents. Curt believes he headed up a drug ring. But Erik, they're wrong. My dad was a loving, generous man. He wouldn't have hurt anyone, especially not Doug O'Sullivan. He loved that man like a brother, and he would have given his life in Doug's place if that would have been possible." She looked up at Erik, seeming to need assurance that he believed her words were true.

"I'll bet he was a great dad."

She dried her tears and nodded. "Yes, he was. I could always count on him to be there for me. No matter how much I messed up. Now there's no one."

"That's not true, Cheryl. I'm here."

She looked at him, narrowing her eyes as if considering the validity of his words. "But you don't even know me."

Erik smiled. "Perhaps I know you better than you give me credit for."

"Why? How? I was stranger to you and your family until last year."

"I don't think there has to be a lot of history between people in order to care for someone. I fly down to Mexico and South America almost every spring or summer with a group of Christian doctors. I help with the lab work and physical therapy, and I find I lose my heart to the people I work with. They need someone to care, and I guess God just gave me the ability to be that person."

Cheryl sat back and folded her hands. "Don't lose your heart to me, Erik Connors. I'm no good, and I know that. The only man who ever really loved me was my father, and apparently, I wasn't enough to keep him here."

"Don't say that," Erik said softly. He turned to read the expression on her face and found such sadness that without thinking he pulled her back against him. "Everyone is deserving of love, and if I want to lose my heart to you, that's my business."

But even as he said it, Erik felt something stir inside. He

was losing his heart to Cheryl. Maybe not falling in love, but in a deep abiding compassion that made him want to protect her from the world and its hurts.

Cheryl said nothing, seeming content to lean against him. Erik wondered how he could persuade her to let him be her friend. Even if friends were all they could ever be, Erik knew that he wanted it more than anything else. "Tell me about your father," he said without thinking.

"He wasn't involved—"

Erik stilled her. "I didn't ask you to defend his position in this mess. I asked you to tell me about him. Tell me what it was like growing up the daughter of Ben Fairchild. Tell me what you loved the most about him."

Cheryl pushed away, and Erik was surprised by the smile on her face. "That's easy. He always believed in me no matter how badly I goofed things up. He was never condemning—oh, maybe now and then. I had some trouble when I moved back here from Los Angeles. He wasn't too happy about my engagement. It was kind of sudden, and I didn't have a good track record with men. So I stayed in one of the downtown hotels and even lived a while with CJ O'Sullivan. I mean Aldersson."

"But you reconciled with your father?"

"Of course," she replied matter-of-factly. "He could never stay upset for long. Pretty soon he was calling me and saying that if I wanted to marry this man, he would have to respect my opinion of him."

"Sounds like he trusted you to be smart."

"Oh, I don't know. Maybe it was just that he loved to indulge me," she said rather sadly. "When my mother died, he had to fill the emptiness with something, and I was just as handy as anything else. He spoiled me and pampered me with all kinds of good things. We traveled and went on shopping sprees, and we always confided our deepest dreams and secrets to each other."

"How was it you ever found the need to leave home?" Erik realized he'd asked a very personal question and quickly added, "I'm sorry. You don't have to answer that."

"It's all right," Cheryl said. She finally appeared calm and collected. "I guess with Daddy's spoiling came his overprotectiveness as well. He was smothering me, and yet, I couldn't bear the idea of hurting him. I told him I was desperate to see the world and try my wings and that I had to leave Denver and get away from the painful memories."

"What memories?"

"CJ and her parents," she said without thinking. "They were in a terrible plane crash, but of course, Curt—" she paused at the name. Drawing a deep breath she continued. "You, no doubt, know all about that."

"Yes."

"Well, CJ became a recluse and withdrew from everyone and everything. Curt and I had broken up. He'd left Denver for parts unknown, and CJ wanted nothing to do with me. Daddy seemed so distraught over Doug and Jan O'Sullivan's deaths that he sort of withdrew as well. He wasn't himself for many years after that.

"Anyway, I convinced him that I needed space to grow up and a different setting in which to have fun. He was so consumed by the business and how to deal with all the problems that he gladly let me go. Well, maybe not gladly. But he gave me an unlimited bank account and access to company jets and housing throughout the world. What girl could have asked for more?"

"It must have seemed quite the fairy tale."

"For a time," Cheryl answered. She looked at him quite seriously and gave him the briefest hint of a smile. "But all good things come to an end, right?"

"Oh, I wouldn't say that. I think some good things go on and on."

"Like your God?"

Erik smiled. "Yes, for one."

Cheryl frowned and looked away. Erik didn't want to do anything to cause her to put up her walls again, and so he directed the conversation back to her childhood. "What do you remember about your dad from when you were small?"

The tension seemed to leave her face. "He was a very busy man, but he always took time out for me. He wasn't perfect. I'm not one of those people who can only remember the good things about a person who's died. He was often absent and often under a great deal of stress, but he was a good man, and I always knew that if I needed him, he would fly from the far corners of the world to be at my side." She smiled. "Mother said he loved us best, but that we weren't as demanding as a new business venture."

Erik chuckled. "I'm sure that's true."

Cheryl went on. "He would make most of my school programs and dance recitals, and when the flying circus really took off and we started doing more and more air shows, Daddy would just pack us along and take us with him. That's how I got to be such good friends with CJ and Curt."

She spoke his name again, only this time she didn't stumble over it, and Erik thought perhaps it was losing its power to haunt her.

They spent most of the afternoon in discussion, and only after noting that the clock was nearing five, did Erik suggest they call for some Chinese takeout and spend the evening together. Cheryl seemed to find this idea acceptable, and with that acceptance came Erik's first real hope. She had opened up to him in a way that he'd only dared to pray for.

When she got up to go wash her face, Erik found himself in immediate prayer. *God, please help me to do the right thing. I care about this woman in a way that I hadn't really expected, but now I know it's true. I'm not in love with her, but I could easily find myself there. She doesn't know You, however, and because of that I can't give her the false illusion that such a thing could ever happen. I know it's wrong to be unequally yoked, and I know from other people just how painful those relationships can be. Please guard us both in this, and don't let us use the other for personal gain or glory.*

"Do you like sweet and sour chicken?"

Erik looked up to find that Cheryl had returned with a cordless phone.

"Sounds good. How about some cashew chicken as well?"

"That would be fine," she said softly, almost shyly. "I'll go look up the number and call it in."

And with that, she was gone again, and Erik could only sit back and contemplate his next move. *Don't lose sight of what you intended to do from the start,* he reminded himself. *Show her the way to God. Show her the love of Jesus.*

eight

Cheryl suddenly knew what it was to be truly paranoid about people and motives. Whenever the doorbell rang, she found herself cringing and seeking shelter in some remote part of the house where no one would see her. She'd admonished Mary, who now came three times a week, to let no one in and to leave the door unanswered.

She also ignored the telephone except when Erik called. She'd allow the answering machine to pick up the calls, and whenever Erik's voice sounded, a feeling of peace seemed to course through her. But the other calls left her frantic and worried. Multiple people called wanting information about her father. Other's, pretending to be some old friend of her father's, called on the pretense of making sure she was all right.

Once, she'd thought the voice of an elderly man sounded familiar and picked up the call only to find that he was actually with one of the rag-mags, those paper tabloids sold in supermarkets everywhere. The man immediately offered her ten thousand dollars for her story, and Cheryl had crashed the receiver down, hoping that the sound had communicated her anger to the man.

From the day of her encounter with the man from the Denver *Post*, Cheryl kept the heavy drapes drawn in every room and the door securely locked. She saw the way her home had turned into a prison of sorts, but it was better than being exposed to prying eyes and the heartlessness of journalists.

Fridays were one of Mary's days off, and with them came a kind of gloom that Cheryl dreaded. Saturday and Sunday were days she'd always spent with her father, and even when she'd been engaged to Grant, she'd tried to keep these days open to catch up with what her father was doing or learn what new adventure he'd involved himself in.

But now he was gone, and Saturday and Sunday were just haunting reminders of his death. Because of this, Friday merely became a prelude to the coming weekend. Sitting in front of the television, Cheryl found herself watching a commercial for baby formula. Tears slid down her cheeks. Once again she remembered what she'd lost.

The only light that had been allowed into the room came by way of the television, and with each changing scene, the shadows on the wall played tricks with Cheryl's imagination. She thought the rocking chair had begun to move, almost as if a ghostly image had taken up residence to keep her company.

"Daddy," she whispered, then the television lighting changed again, and she could see that the chair was quite empty.

Pressing her hands to her head, Cheryl thought perhaps she was going crazy. The sound of children laughing on the television made her stop up her ears and cry even harder. The sound of her heart pounded in her closed ears.

Ba-bom. . .ba-bom. . .ba-bom.

She imagined it slowing, weakening, growing steadily silent. She pictured it stopping altogether and of herself laying dead on the couch. There was no sense in existing when all she felt was pain. The misery threatened her by the minute anyway, so why not give into it and end her life? Then they'd all be sorry they'd made her suffer.

Cheryl sobered and switched off the television. It wasn't

like she hadn't considered suicide before. Her father had taken that way out, so it seemed only appropriate that she do the same. After all, if she was expected to forgive him his choice, surely he would forgive her choosing the same.

"Don't hate me, Daddy," she whispered, looking upward. "Don't hate me because I'm weak. You were the strongest man I knew, and you couldn't stand up under the pressure of life, so why should I have to?"

"Cheryl!" a masculine voice called out.

She started, not expecting to hear her own name being called. It was only then that she realized someone was pounding on the front door. The doorbell sounded, echoing through the silent house. This was followed again with the calling of her name. She strained to hear without leaving her sanctuary. The voice sounded vaguely familiar, yet she knew it wasn't Erik.

"Cheryl, open up. It's Curt!"

Her heart raced. Curt? Curt was here?

She moved toward the threshold and gripped the wall for extra support. She felt her knees grow weak, and her legs felt all rubbery. Curt was here, and he wouldn't leave until she opened the door and allowed him and his painful reminders to enter her privacy.

The pounding sounded again.

"Cheryl, I'll break this door down if I have to. You know me well enough to know that I'm speaking the truth."

She found herself actually smiling at this. Curt would do just what he'd said. She had little doubt about it. Curt could get blood out of turnips, as the old saying was so fond of pointing out.

Swallowing hard, she moved silently toward the door and put her hand out to touch the heavy oak. Curt pounded against it again, and Cheryl allowed the vibrations to shake through her. When it stopped, she turned the lock and knew that he would realize that once again he had won. She tried to imagine the look of sheer satisfaction on his face as they met eye to eye.

Turning the dead bolt, she glanced down momentarily to find that she was a mess, as usual. She'd thrown on her father's old, worn sweats and one of his T-shirts. The sweats had been cinched with their drawstring in order to keep them from falling off Cheryl's slender frame, and they ballooned out in a bulky fashion. She hadn't even bothered to brush her hair or put on makeup, and the thought of facing Curt in such a state seemed awkward. Not that she cared what he thought, but he knew how good she could look when she wanted to.

With one last deep breath, she opened the door and squinted against the brilliance of the noontime sun.

"What do you want?" she asked in a harsh monotone.

"Good grief, Cheryl," Curt said, without seeming the least bit concerned for her feelings. "What have you done to yourself? Or maybe I should ask, what have you neglected to do for yourself?"

Cheryl looked at him hard and tried to put aside her rage. If she lost control, Curt would only use it against her. Of this, she was certain.

"You aren't welcome here," she replied. "I think you know that, too."

Curt shrugged. "I'm on DEA business, and whether you like it or not, you have to deal with me." He glanced behind him for a moment, then faced her again. "Unless of course, you have my nosey brother-in-law hiding out in the house, ready to whisk you away from this confrontation."

Cheryl stepped back from the door and walked away. "Do what you have to," she called over her shoulder.

Curt followed her into the living room, and the first thing he did was throw open the drapes.

"Don't do that," Cheryl protested. "I don't need to have people spying on me."

"It's as dark as a tomb in here," Curt answered, allowing light to pour through yet another window.

"That's the way I want it." She plopped down into a wing-backed chair, giving him no chance to sit close to her. "My house. My tomb."

"There, that's better," he said, seeming to ignore her.

Cheryl noticed for the first time that he was dressed in navy slacks and a beige and navy pullover shirt. *He looks rather nice*, she thought. Just like he always did. Not at all like a murderer.

He caught her staring at him and smiled. "I'm still the same old Curt, if that's what you're wondering. I didn't suddenly grow horns and a tail, just because of what happened." He sat in another of the wing-backed chairs and leaned forward. "I want you to know how sorry I am that things have to be the way they are."

Her defenses went securely into place. "No, you aren't," she barely whispered. "You are on a personal vendetta, and I can only hope that your series of killings will eventually include me."

Curt's mouth dropped open, but no words came out. *Good*, Cheryl thought, *let him think on that one for a while.*

"Did you never happen to think about the pain you were inflicting? Didn't you ever wonder what the results of your meddling might be?" she questioned, looking at him with an unemotional expression. "Poor Curtiss O'Sullivan. He had to be a big man and prove to the world that his father was still a great flyer. No pilot error could be attributed to the great Douglas O'Sullivan's crash. No, better to make up a story about cocaine and corrupt business partners. Better to push old men into death and eliminate anyone else who got in the way, including unborn infants. No telling what that baby might have grown up to do for his or her own method of revenge against the O'Sullivan family."

She fell silent and crossed her arms against her chest. She watched Curt with a need to memorize everything about him. Her anger needed to be fed with the vision of the man who had caused her misery.

"Are you done?" he asked softly.

"Are you?" she countered without missing a beat.

Curt shifted uncomfortably and shook his head. "Not until this is completely resolved."

"What's the matter? Your list of victims still too short?" Her voice was heavily laden with sarcasm. The anger was surfacing against her will. "Hey, did you bring your gun? Maybe you could just go ahead and do me in right now. You want me to run? I could run," she said, getting to her feet. "That way it will look just as justifiable as the other killings."

"Sit down, Cheryl, and knock it off." Curt's voice was demanding, and his expression had changed to one of determined purpose.

"Oh," she said, sitting back down, "do you need a more steady target? That's right, Grant wasn't running when you killed him. Hey, neither was I. I just happened to get in the way. It really is a shame that you had the paramedics so close on hand. You killed my baby, but just didn't have enough luck to take us both out at the same time. Now you have to waste another bullet. Pity. Do they cost a lot? Maybe I could reimburse you."

"Stop it!" he exclaimed getting to his feet. He crossed the

small space between them and leaned over her, putting his hands on the armrests on either side of her. "Stop it now! I'm not going to listen to this anymore. I'm here to do my job and investigate you like I would any other suspect."

"So I'm a suspect, now?" she said, staring him in the eye. Blink for blink, she kept her expression fixed.

Curt calmed a bit and straightened. "Yes."

Cheryl could see the anguish in his eyes. She'd really hurt him and it was easy to see that it had taken its toll on his composure. *Good. I hope it hurts a lot*, she thought. *I hope it hurts you like it hurts me.*

Curt retook his seat before continuing. "There are things which I hope you can clarify for me. Things which actually might take the heat off your father's involvement."

"What, and put it on Grant?" she asked angrily. "Of course, both men are dead so you might as well blame one as blame the other. Neither one can defend himself."

Curt sighed heavily. "I'm not trying to assign blame. I'm looking for the truth."

"Your truth," she replied, this time lowering her voice. "The kind of truth that wipes out the innocent and destroys all hope."

"Cheryl, I never meant for you or your unborn baby to get hurt. I never meant for Ben to die. I won't apologize for Grant, however. He pulled the gun first and shot first, and he put your life in danger, as well as Christy's and his own daughter's. Why is it so impossible for you to see that he didn't care who he killed or hurt, so long as he protected his shipment of cocaine?"

Cheryl remembered what Erik had pointed out about Grant deliberately shooting her in the stomach. She felt some of the fight go out from her as she noted the sincerity in Curt's eyes. This was Curt, the man she'd once loved. A man she knew better than many. She shook her head. No, she didn't know him at all. He was a killer, and he had ruined her life.

"Cheryl, I'm not without feeling, and if you'll recall, the first deaths related to this case were my own mother and father. You can deny that possibility all you want, but the evidence was there and in place. Ben managed to get the matter swept under the rug in order to protect himself."

"Stop bad-mouthing my father," she said coolly. Forcing a calm to counter Curt's sympathetic speech, she continued, "You know very well that I cared greatly what happened to your parents. You are the one who shut me out and left for parts unknown after breaking our engagement. You were the one who deserted CJ when she needed you most, so please don't tell me how much you care."

Curt ran a hand through his hair. "Yes, I did desert you both when you needed me, but I couldn't deal with the situation, and I had to find a way to expose the truth. In my own youthful exuberance, I thought it might honestly be the only way to make things right again. I know now that it doesn't matter how people hate or how much anger they allow to control their actions. It doesn't bring dead bodies back to life. It didn't for me, and it won't for you either."

Cheryl felt her breath catch at the truth in his words. She didn't want to listen to any more. She didn't want to believe Curt really cared.

"So why are you here? What is it you expect from me? If it's a confession, I hate to disappoint you, but I don't have one."

"I'm here to ask you about what you do have. You have memories of things your father might have said or done. You may even know where he's left vital information. We both need this matter settled, Cheryl. In case you didn't know it, the assets for O&F Aviation are frozen, and it's only a matter of time until you find yourself without any means of support."

Cheryl instantly thought of the fifty thousand dollars hidden in the lockbox. The lockbox! Eyeing Curt suspiciously, she questioned, "What kind of information do you mean?"

Curt seemed to relax a bit. "We're hoping there's paperwork. You know, something that might list buyers, sellers, drug exchange locations. Do you have any idea where such information might be kept?"

"Why should I?"

"I thought maybe Ben might have a special place in the house for keeping things he didn't want anyone else to get ahold of."

"You're that certain my father was the mastermind of your little drug ring?"

Curt shook his head. "I'm not certain of anything except what Ben told me."

"Which was?"

"That Grant forced him into the situation. It seems Grant found problems in the accounting department and threatened to expose O&F Aviation to the Internal Revenue Service if Ben didn't cooperate."

"I don't believe you," Cheryl said flatly.

"I don't much care. I know what Ben said, and I know, too, that he had a part in the plane crash that killed my parents. He told me so."

"No way!" she yelled, getting to her feet. "There is no way my father had anything to do with that. He wouldn't have been able to live with himself all these years."

Curt, too, got to his feet. "Cheryl, didn't it ever dawn on you that it was that which caused your father to act so strangely after the crash? By your own admission, Ben changed after my parents died. He took the crash very hard, you said. Isn't it possible that it wasn't just because friends had died, but because he had a hand in their death?"

"How dare you! Get out of my house!"

"You have to listen to reason Cheryl, or you may find yourself behind bars. I'm having this house searched from top to bottom, and there's nothing you can do about it."

"Did you forget your buddies already took care of that while I was in the hospital?"

"It doesn't matter. We'll do it again. We'll do it over and over if it means that there is even the most remote possibility of finding the truth."

Cheryl turned away from him and crossed the room. "Until you show up with a search warrant, you can get out of my house. You've done me enough damage, Curt. I hardly think it fair that I should have to be confronted by my baby's killer. Why don't you send someone else next time?"

"Someone else might not be as generous as me," Curt said seriously. He came to stand beside her, and his expression softened in a way that Cheryl would just as soon forget. "Cheryl, I know you're hurting. I didn't stop caring about you just because I became a DEA officer and married Christy. You're like a part of the family to me. Don't shut me out."

Cheryl shook her head. "I'm nothing to you, and you're nothing to me. If you want to care, that's your problem, but maybe a better way of showing it would be to just stay away from me."

Curt sighed. "I'll go for now, but I'll be back later. Don't even think of not answering the door. I think you know me well enough to know that a locked door won't keep me out."

"Yes, I'm sure you'll plow right through any obstacle in order to get what you want," she answered, barely able to keep her anger in check.

She walked to the door and opened it for him. The sunlight didn't blind her as before, but the heat of the day hit her like a blast from a hot furnace. Stepping back, she let Curt pass. Curt turned to face her as if to say something more, but Cheryl read an instant sorrow in his expression that forced her to see his feelings were genuine. *I don't care*, she reasoned. *I don't care how sorry he is.*

"Cheryl," he began, "I hope that somehow, one day, you will forgive me my part in this. I hope that one day you'll understand my need for the truth."

"The truth is that you have ended my life in every way but one. I don't know how you live with what you've done. I don't know how you sleep nights or look at yourself in the mirror without wanting to put a gun to your head for the things you, alone, are responsible for." She saw his shoulders slump a bit and noted that his eyes grew moist. She hated him for making her feel like an ogre, but she pressed home her final point. "I'll never forgive you for killing the people I loved most, and I'll never forgive you for putting me through this misery."

nine

"Mary," Cheryl began, coming into the kitchen, "I need for you to do an errand for me. Do you mind?"

The older woman straightened from where she was bent over the dishwasher, stacking dirty dishes. "Not at all, Cheryl. What do you need?"

"I want you to go to the bank for me and see about cashing this check. I have no idea if this account if frozen or not, and I certainly don't want to call up and ask. I'm afraid that would only lead to them becoming suspicious if it's not."

Mary nodded. "What should I do?"

"Just take it to a teller and ask to cash it. Since it's drawn on that bank, they'll be able to access the account immediately, and there shouldn't be any problem. Unless," she paused, biting at her lower lip, "unless the account is frozen to my use."

Mary closed the dishwasher and pulled off her apron. "And if they will cash it?"

Cheryl handed her the check. "If they will cash it, there's enough there to stock up on groceries, pay your salary, and keep a little cash in the house."

"Do you want me to go ahead and stop by the store on my way back?"

Cheryl nodded. "That would be great."

Mary gathered her things up and let herself out the back door. "There's an omelette on the warming tray," she said nonchalantly. "Don't forget to eat it."

Cheryl knew Mary would only make a big deal of things if she didn't eat, so rather than argue, she went immediately to the tray and pulled out the plate. "Looks good, Mary. I'll eat it right now." The old woman nodded approvingly and closed the door.

Cheryl picked up a fork and began to eat. At first she just picked around the edges, but soon the aroma and the taste made her hungry for more, and she polished it off in record time. In the old days before her father's death, worry had always given her a ravenous appetite. That, in turn, had given her more than a little bit of a battle to keep her rather voluptuous figure neat and trim. Now she was downright skinny, and the look was not good on her.

She paced the kitchen for a few minutes before deciding on a glass of orange juice. Would Mary be able to cash the check? Curt had warned her that sooner or later her money would be tight due to the feds putting a hold on her financial affairs. *Thank goodness he didn't know about the fifty grand*, she thought. That would be her salvation, thanks to her father's foresight. Still, she would have to be careful. Fifty thousand was a mere drop in the bucket compared to what she was used to having at her disposal. She immediately set her mind to ways of economizing and had just headed to her father's study when she heard the unmistakable roar of Erik's truck.

Going to the window, she pulled back the curtain enough to assure herself that it was him, and him alone, before opening the door.

"Erik, what a surprise." And for once, it seemed quite nice to have him show up unexpectedly.

"I tried to call, but they said your number had been disconnected. Is everything okay?"

"Not disconnected, just changed and unlisted," she said

and motioned him inside. "Might as well come in since you're already here."

Erik grinned. "I'm not imposing?"

"Would it matter?" she asked with the slightest hint of good-natured teasing to her voice.

"Nope, not a bit."

"I didn't think so," she answered, and this time there followed a smile. "Come on in."

Cheryl led him to the family room and offered him a seat. "I suppose you heard about Curt's interview with me last week?"

Erik shook his head. "Curt's not telling me anything. I think I've been branded a traitor in the camp. After I came clean with him about sneaking you off that first time, he hasn't been too inclined to include me in his moves."

Cheryl curled up on the sofa and considered this for a moment. "I was pretty hard on him, but he deserved it. He has to know that his little game has hurt a great many people. I just didn't want to be bothered any more by it, and yet he storms into my house and demands that I remember the very things I'd gone out of my way to forget."

"Is that why you changed your telephone number?"

"That and the twenty to thirty calls I was getting from complete strangers. Most wanted to do an interview with me and just came right out and left a message on the machine. Others were more subtle. I've had calls from so many so-called 'friends of the family' that I was ready to scream. I've had calls from doctors, lawyers, politicians, security people, and a dozen others, all who professed to be deeply concerned, old friends of Dad who wanted to lend me support in my hour of need."

"Maybe they were legitimate," Erik suggested.

"Not a chance. Daddy didn't have that many friends. He

was too cautious after losing Doug and Jan O'Sullivan and. . ." She paused to take a long drink of the juice before adding, "my mother."

"But surely there were some of those who actually thought themselves to be friends," Erik replied. "Maybe they really were concerned about your well-being."

"Maybe," she said with a shrug, "but they were nowhere around when he killed himself four months ago. It wasn't until the DEA case was revealed and the shoot-out took place that any of this sudden interest in my well-being started up."

Erik nodded. "I guess I can see where you'd be skeptical."

Cheryl found herself relaxing in Erik's presence. It was strange, she thought, but he made her feel as though no one else in the world cared quite as much as he did. He made her realize that she didn't have to be alone, and yet, he was also mixed up in the whole affair.

"So how did your interview with Curt go?" Erik suddenly asked.

"Miserably, as I knew it would. Curt only wants to believe the worst about my father."

"Whereas you only want to believe the best?" he asked with a hesitant smile.

She nodded. "I suppose that's one way of putting it. And why not? I loved my father and will always love him. I don't want to see his memory dragged through the mud while Curt gets his revenge for something that might have been a total accident."

"But you can't be sure that what he suspects isn't dead to rights. Didn't he admit that your father told him of his involvement with the drug ring?"

Cheryl bristled at this. She wanted Erik to be a friend, not another adversary. "Those are Curt's words. I don't believe them for even one minute."

"Then why would your father kill himself? He seemed for all purposes to have the world by the tail. Why would all of the sudden death be preferable to life? Then too, you have to admit there was something going on between him and Grant. After all, Grant was working for your father under an assumed name."

Cheryl gulped down the remaining orange juice and tried to steady her nerves. "I know it looks bad." She fell silent for a few moments, then surprised both herself and Erik by asking, "What was Grant really like? I mean the Grant who was married to your sister?"

Erik's eyes widened for a moment. "He was the king of deception. I doubt seriously that he was ever faithful to Candy, and I still have a hard time figuring out why he even involved himself with her. Curt thinks it might have been as simple as the fact that he wanted to stay close to Christy's dress design business so that he could continue to import drugs through her warehouses. I'd like to believe that at one point he really did love her, for whatever reason. But I don't think he did. He was a user, Cheryl. He made Christy pay for Candy's hospital bills, and he insisted on money from Christy in order to 'buy' Sarah's adoption from him."

Cheryl tried to imagine that it was all true. Erik had no reason to lie to her, and yet she wanted so much for the entire matter to be a terrible mistake.

"He didn't want Sarah?" Cheryl asked, hesitantly.

"No. He told Candy that children were a complication to life that he didn't need. He was angry when she told him that she was already pregnant. I know, because I was there when she broke the news to all of us."

"He wasn't happy about our baby, either," she said in a whisper. She could remember only too well what he'd been like when he found out. He'd accused her of trying to step up the wedding before he was ready. He'd said she had set a trap for him, and he didn't necessarily have to fall into it.

"It all figures," Erik said, seeming to sense her turmoil. "Grant had too many other irons in the fire. Children would have just interfered with his plans for quick breaks and easy getaways."

"But he married your sister," she replied flatly. "For some reason, it was important enough for him to tie himself that much."

"But what's a wife? It isn't like he'd have to arrange for her care if he should suddenly need to flee the country. He could just as easily divorce her from far away, as to stay here and be married. A child, however, would be an entirely different matter."

"Even if that was the real way Grant operated," she said, trying hard to put the pieces together, "my father was an honorable man. He was good and kind, and I know he could never have been capable of the things Curt has accused him of."

"Fathers don't always turn out the way we'd like them to be."

Cheryl frowned. "What's that supposed to mean?"

Erik shrugged. "We'd all like to believe the best about our parents, but sometimes it just isn't possible. Sometimes, our parents are the first ones to dispel the myths surrounding them."

"Is that how your parents were?" she asked. Suddenly she realized that she knew nothing about Erik and his childhood.

Erik's face contorted as if the pain of answering such a question had become too much. "My parents definitely dispelled any myths I had formulated in my mind."

"How?"

"My father, in particular, was a ruthless man. He did whatever he had to do, walked over whoever he had to walk over, all in order to get things his own way. He was unfaithful in every single relationship I ever saw him have. And that included those with my mother and sisters."

"What about your relationship with him?"

"Especially mine," he said and took a deep breath. "The man's corrupt, and he corrupts everything he touches. He uses people to get what he wants, and then he throws them away as though they were nothing more than wrappings on Christmas presents."

Cheryl frowned. Hadn't she done much the same in life? She knew that she could be ruthless when the situation presented itself. She had been heartless where Curt was concerned and had gone out of her way to say the most hurtful, mean-spirited things she could think of. She felt hot tears form in her eyes, but Erik didn't seem to notice them.

"I hated him for a long time. It took coming to God and begging Him to take the anger and rage from within me. I still can't say that I miss him or have any desire to see him, but I no longer hate him like I did."

Cheryl sniffed back tears, and Erik seemed to notice for the first time that she was crying. "I'm sorry," he said very softly. "I didn't mean to upset you."

His kindness only made matters worse. Cheryl began to cry in earnest. "I'm just as bad," she finally managed to say. "I've used people and walked over them on my way to the top. Grant was the only man I couldn't wrap around my finger and manipulate in the manner to which I was accustomed. He became a challenge and I took the bait without considering the cost. I threw myself into harm's way over and over again, and all in order to have my own way," her voice was ragged with sorrow. "You must hate me. I sound just like your father."

Erik got up from his chair and came to sit beside her on the couch. "There's a great difference between you and my father," he said, putting his arm around her shoulder. With great tenderness, he lifted her face to meet his.

"There is?" she said, wishing against all odds that he was speaking the truth.

"Absolutely. My father has never once been repentant of his actions," Erik said quite seriously. "Where as with you, I see nothing but regret and the desire to be free from the part you once played. That woman doesn't live inside you anymore."

"How can you be so sure?" she asked, choking back a sob.

Erik smiled, and it gave her such warmth and hope that she wanted to throw herself against him and hang onto him as though he alone could show her the way to peace.

"I see it in your eyes," he replied. "I see it in your face, even though you try to keep your mask in place. I even see it in your actions. You've rid yourself of the clothes which once represented your lifestyle. Your clothes and hair and all that goes with them were visual symbols of what existed in the past. When you finally realize that they didn't truly make the woman, you won't be so afraid to go back to wearing nice things.

"But I also know that you won't return to the lifestyle you lived back then. You've seen too much, and you know too much to go back and pretend that it doesn't hurt any-one—that it doesn't hurt you." He paused and let go of her face. "I think if you give it some thought, Cheryl, you'll see for yourself that it's true."

She continued to look at him for several moments before speaking. "There's nothing back there for me. That woman is dead, or should be."

"No," Erik replied and his voice held unmistakable tenderness. "That woman needs to live again, but not in the old way. She needs to repent and find peace with God and to realize that she isn't alone. The Bible says that when we come to accept God, we become new creatures and the old is cast off. Wouldn't you like that assurance for yourself?"

Cheryl felt goose bumps form on her arms. Erik had opened a door that she'd thought forever closed to her. The only question now, was whether she'd ever have the courage to cross the threshold.

ten

"I'm really glad you agreed to talk to me," CJ Aldersson said, taking a seat in the living room.

Cheryl attempted a smile and took a place on the sofa. "I figured you weren't going to give up."

"You didn't give up on me."

"Yes, I did," Cheryl stated quite seriously. "When I grew tired of being unable to help you after the plane crash, I took off for Europe. Then when I came back to Denver and made plans for marriage to Strat—Grant, well I could see that you needed a great deal of help, and again I didn't know what to do."

"But you didn't stop caring about me, did you?"

Cheryl studied CJ for a moment and considered her question in earnest. For far too long she'd given flippant answers and generalized speeches. Always, she kept in mind what people wanted to hear, and somehow she managed to play the game and tell them what they needed her to say. But no more. She was determined to be honest and straightforward.

"No, I didn't stop caring," she admitted, "but I replaced the importance of our friendship with other things."

"What about now?" CJ asked, pushing back her shoulder-length, copper hair.

Cheryl shook her head. "I don't know, and that's the honest truth. I'm afraid to care about anyone, and I can't let go of my anger at Curt."

"But you loved him once. Can't you draw on that for the

moment and remember the good things about him? Can't you try to realize how important it is for him to resolve this situation?"

"But at what cost, CJ? Where do you stop? Curt's need to resolve the situation, as you put it, has taken its toll of victims."

"Why can't you see that Curt never created the victims to start with?" CJ's voice took on a hard edge. "Cheryl, I'm going to tell you something that I never thought I would."

Cheryl watched her friend twist her hands together as if seeking some kind of inner strength.

"When the plane went down the night of the crash, my father turned to my mother. With sadness that was born out of the reality of what was about to happen, he said, 'He's done us in.' My mother's response was rather muffled, and for years I thought she'd replied, 'In?' Now I know that she wasn't saying 'in,' but rather 'Ben.' My father nodded in affirmation. You see, he knew Ben had some part in it because he'd just talked to him before leaving the airport. He'd found cocaine on one of the O&F planes and Ben had told him to mind his own business, or threatened him, or whatever else you want to imagine. We'll never know because my father carried it to the grave, and your father didn't say a whole lot about it."

Cheryl refrained from demanding that CJ leave the house. She felt confused by her friend's statement. It was as if forces were joining together to show her a side of her father that she'd never believed existed.

"I don't want you to feel bad or hate anyone, Cheryl," CJ continued. "I really don't. I no longer feel angry with Ben or, for that matter, Grant. To hate either one or to allow the bitterness of the past to take hold would be to give in to the evil of this entire situation. God doesn't want that for me, and He doesn't want that for you."

"I don't know what to think any more," Cheryl finally said, laying her head back to stare at the ceiling. "Everyone keeps coming to me to show me these things about my father. Things that I can't believe, yet things which are hard to deny. I just know how he felt about us. How much he loved me and my mother, and how much he loved your father. I can't see him jeopardizing that respect and love for a few extra dollars in drug money."

"But Curt says that Ben explained his predicament, and while it doesn't justify his actions, it certainly shows that your father wasn't just in it for the money."

"And how is that?"

"Ben accidentally fell behind in some bookkeeping, and when it was discovered, O&F owed the IRS over a million dollars in back taxes. The IRS didn't know this, however, and when Grant found out the mistake had been made, he went to Ben and proposed a deal. Ben had little choice. Either he would bury the company in a financial crisis that would probably result in him having to file bankruptcy, or he could go along with Grant's request. My thoughts are that he didn't want to lose my father's respect, nor did he want the public shame and humiliation that would be brought down on them. You know for yourself that appearance was everything to Ben."

Cheryl slowly looked back at CJ and nodded. "He wanted to make a statement to the world. I guess he's done just that."

CJ crossed her legs and relaxed against the back of the chair. "Cheryl, please don't shut me out anymore. I'm not the enemy, and neither is Curt. Don't you want to know the truth? Wouldn't you rather have all slates be wiped clean?"

"Even if it means that my father's name is forever tarnished?"

"Do you think if you don't cooperate and remain bitterly hateful that you will stop the progress of this investigation? Don't you realize that with or without you, they will come to the truth?"

Cheryl shrugged. "At least without me, I won't be a traitor to Dad."

"How does being truthful make you a traitor?" CJ questioned softly.

Tucking her jean-clad legs under her, Cheryl released a heavy sigh. "I don't know. I don't know much of anything anymore."

"Then know this. I'm your friend, and I care about you. I will always be here for you."

Cheryl felt her eyes grow moist. *I will not cry*, she admonished herself. "I'm not worthy of your friendship," she told CJ quite honestly. "The things I've done—the person I am. I don't deserve friends or love."

"Nonsense," CJ replied, shaking her head. "That simply isn't true. There is no one whom God can't forgive, and if we are to follow His example, then we much forgive each other and ourselves, as well."

Cheryl regained her composure before answering. CJ's words so clearly mirrored the things Erik had told her that deep within, she found herself actually hoping against the odds that they was true.

"I don't know if I can forgive," Cheryl replied. "I don't know if I want to forgive."

CJ nodded. "I think I can understand, maybe not in full, but at least enough to know that what you say is born of pain and loss. Just promise me that you'll think about what I've said and that you'll give God a chance to reveal Himself to you."

"That much I can do," Cheryl answered.

Just then the doorbell sounded and both women jumped in surprise. Cheryl went to the window and saw that a dark-headed man in a business suit stood outside her door.

"I don't know who it is," she said, coming back to where CJ sat. "I get some pretty weird people from time to time. They want interviews or exclusive information about the case, and so most of the time, I don't even open the door."

"Would you like me to answer it?" CJ asked, getting to her feet.

"Would you?"

"Sure." CJ went to the door while Cheryl waited in hiding around the foyer wall. "Can I help you?" she heard CJ question.

"I'm with the DEA," the man said. "Damon Brooks is my name, and I'm here to speak with Ms. Fairchild. Is that you?"

"No, I'm CJ Aldersson, her friend."

"I'm Cheryl Fairchild," Cheryl said, coming into the foyer. "What do you want?"

"I need to ask you some information."

"I just talked to Curt O'Sullivan last week."

The man seemed not in the least bit fazed by this information. "As I said, ma'am, I need to talk to you."

"Then I suppose you should come in," Cheryl replied and turned to CJ. "Can you stay?"

"Absolutely."

The three made their way into the living room where CJ and Cheryl sat together on the couch, while Damon Brooks took a seat in one of the wing-backed chairs. He took out a pad of paper and a pen, before turning a glaring look on Cheryl.

"We need your father's list of contacts," he said abruptly.

It was exactly what Curt had asked for when he'd been

there, and Cheryl shook her head. "I don't know about any list of contacts."

"Come now, Ms. Fairchild." The man's irritation grew quite apparent. "Withholding evidence is only going to dig you in deeper."

Cheryl felt her face flush. "I'm not in this thing, no matter how much you want to put me there."

"You can't expect us to believe that. You were the mistress of Grant Burks, one of the key players, and you were the daughter of Ben Fairchild. We have enough information to see you sent to prison for a very long time."

"But I haven't done anything, except perhaps—" She stopped and glance momentarily at CJ, "Except love the wrong people."

"I'm not playing games with you, lady. You may have thought you could get away with this kind of thing with O'Sullivan, but you are dealing with a completely different man now."

"Is that any reason to be rude and uncivil?" CJ interjected, eyeing the man with a look of severity.

"You related to this case?" Brooks asked angrily.

"Yes, as a matter of fact, I am. I'm CJ Aldersson, and my brother is Curt O'Sullivan. We are co-owners in O&F Aviation with Miss Fairchild."

The man noted this on paper, while posing yet another question. "Do you know anything about a list of contacts and exchange locations?

"No," CJ replied flatly.

Cheryl felt relief that the pressure was off her even for a few moments. She thought of the papers in the lockbox and realized that they had to be exactly what the DEA was looking for. She thought about producing the goods, then decided against it. What if the papers showed her father to truly have been the mastermind behind the entire drug operation? Could she bear up under that kind of truth? Could she stand by and see his memory forever scarred?

"I don't think you're listening to me, Ms. Fairchild." The man leaned forward aggressively.

His action caused Cheryl to grow quite angry. No one came into her house and made threatening motions and got away with it. Standing up, she proclaimed, "As I told Curt, I have nothing to say or to show or to share. You aren't welcome in this house, and the sooner you get it through your heads, the better."

The man jumped to his feet and pushed Cheryl backward, shocking both women. He reached out as if to take hold of her, and Cheryl fought back by slapping the man's arms until finally he stilled her with a vicious hold. His iron-clad grip threatened to break her bones. Cheryl winced in pain, and he yanked her to her feet.

"You'd better get it through your head that we mean business. You have something we want, and we aren't going to lie down and play dead just because you tell us to."

"Leave her alone!" CJ declared. "You have no right to handle her in that fashion."

"This is nothing compared to what I'm going to do if she doesn't come clean."

Now Cheryl was truly sorry she'd demanded Curt to send someone else in his stead. She was frightened by the dark eyes of the stranger. There was an underlying hatred in his expression, and he seemed to take great joy in hurting her.

Twisting her wrists outward, Cheryl screamed in pain while CJ, unable to stand anymore of it, got up from her chair and went to the telephone.

"What do you think you're doing?" the man demanded.

"I'm calling my brother. Your actions are unacceptable, and no DEA agent has the right to treat another person this way."

The man laughed in stilted amusement. "If you don't want me to break your friend's arms, you'll put the phone down and sit yourself back on that couch."

CJ held the phone for a moment. She seemed to weigh the validity of his threat before returning the receiver to its cradle. "Very well. But you won't get away with this, Mr. Brooks. I'll see you brought up on charges of harassment and conduct unbefitting an officer of the law."

The man suddenly pushed Cheryl backward. She fought to regain her balance, but it was useless. She fell against the sofa and struggled to compose herself. Terror gripped her like an iron binding. She could hardly breath for fear of what the man might do next.

"I'm going to search this house, and there's nothing you can do to stop me."

"Without a search warrant," Cheryl said, suddenly allowing her anger to make her brave, "you aren't going to do anything of the kind."

Just then Mary could be heard coming into the house through the kitchen door. "Cheryl!" she called, "I'm here." She entered the room and frowned at the sight. "Am I interrupting?"

"Mary, call the police!" Cheryl declared, and the man seemed to realize he was suddenly dealing with more than he had asked for.

"There's no need for that," Damon Brooks said. "I will return with your precious search warrant. Until then, don't even think of removing evidence from this house. You're being watched, and it would give me extreme pleasure to apprehend you for failure to disclose criminal evidence."

With that he left, slamming the door behind him, leaving the three women to stare after him as if they'd just witnessed some unbelievable apparition. Cheryl began to tremble, and her teeth rattled together nosily.

"I'm going to have a few words with Curt about this," CJ said, getting to her feet. "If the DEA thinks they can come in and break people's bones in order to conjure up confessions, they have another thing coming."

Mary stared at both women in complete confusion. "What happened?"

"I. . .I. . .don't wa. . .want to talk about it," Cheryl stammered.

"Suffice it to say, Mary," CJ said, moving to the foyer, "the DEA got a little out of hand. Cheryl, I'd keep the door locked if I were you. I know you have to deal with these investigations, but I'd make sure someone was here to protect you."

Cheryl immediately thought of Erik, but there was no way she was going to call him and ask him to camp out on her doorstep. No matter how appealing the thought might be.

eleven

Boom!

Cheryl awoke just before dawn to a late summer thunderstorm in full progress. The flashes of lightning lit the room up as though it were daylight, and with each flash came an ear-splitting crash of thunder. The windowpane rattled mercilessly and barely had time to stop vibrating before the next strike came.

Sitting up and hugging her knees to her chest, Cheryl remembered how frightened she'd been of storms as a child. "Think of something pleasant," her mother would say. But for Cheryl there were so many unpleasant things to dwell upon that the pleasant ones didn't stand a chance.

Glancing at the clock on her nightstand, she saw the red illuminated numbers and read 5:45. *It will soon be light*, she thought and decided to go ahead and start the day. The storm would surely seem less menacing if she dressed and busied herself. She went to find her standard wardrobe, T-shirt and jeans, but suddenly felt compelled to do something with her hair. She studied it in the mirror for a moment. The golden ash of her blond hair seemed dingy against her pale skin. When had she last washed it? She couldn't remember.

That determined her first order of business, and despite the fact that a thunderstorm raged on around her, Cheryl stepped into a steaming shower.

The water ran down over her head, penetrating the layers of dirty blond curls, saturating her dry, abused skin. It felt better than Cheryl could ever remember a shower feeling. She lathered her hair and scrubbed until her head ached from the attention. She rinsed this out and lathered again— determined to wash away even the remotest particle of dirt. With this accomplished, she poured on expensive conditioner and massaged her hair the way her hairdresser Michelle had told her to do. *Good grief*, she thought, *Michelle must think I fell off the face of the earth.*

"I guess in a way, I did," she mused aloud. Some people sang in the shower, but Cheryl had always been given to having full conversations with herself.

"I should make an appointment to have my hair cut." She held up the limp lengthy curls and sighed. There had been a time when she'd been a regular every week at the beauty salon.

"What have I done to myself?" she questioned, knowing full well the answer. She'd given up on life, but slowly through the efforts of her friends, and even her enemies, Cheryl realized that just because she wanted life to end was no sure sign that it would. She picked up a plush washcloth and soap and began to wash her body, thinking as she did that she needed to somehow find her way back among the living.

"But I don't feel alive," she said and passed the cloth over her stomach. She remembered the baby, something that happened at the strangest moments. As usual, tears came unbidden to her eyes. Why was this so hard to get past? It was just a baby. An unborn fetus without a name or, for all she knew, sex.

But wait, didn't her obstetrician tell her that the sex of the baby could be determined early on? She had been well into her fourth month when the shooting took place. Why had she never thought to ask about the sex of her miscarried child? Beyond that, what had happened to her baby? She shuddered to think of it joining a pile of aborted fetuses. Those babies had also been murdered, as far as she considered it, but they hadn't been wanted, and hers had been.

So many questions came to mind, and her thoughts blocked out any fear of the storm. She would call her doctor as soon as the office was open and see if the records showed what the sex of her baby had been. It seemed to comfort her to imagine that within hours she would know if she'd lost a son or daughter. These thoughts made a normal progression to the desire to name her unborn child and maybe even erect a memorial stone beside her father's grave in honor of the baby no one would ever know.

Cheryl finished the shower with a new, determined purpose. It wasn't until she'd stepped out and was toweling herself off that she noticed the tile that safety hid her father's lockbox. She pulled on her robe and went to pry open the tile. The need to review the contents of the box was strong. Mary had been able to cash her check, but Cheryl wondered how long those funds would hold out. She couldn't have more than six or seven thousand dollars in that account, and there was no way of knowing whether she could access money from any of the other accounts.

She pulled out the lockbox and took it the bathroom vanity. Since she'd pried the lock once before, it now wanted to stick and refuse her admission. She opened the drawer and found a pair of styling scissors which she immediately lodged between the metal frame of the box in order to force it open once again.

Pop! The noise startled her as the lid sprang back and slapped against the countertop.

The money stared up at her like a faithful reminder of her father. Maybe he had known all along that she'd have need of this money. Maybe he'd figured he might need it himself. She fingered it gently, reassuring herself that she'd not be destitute if the bank refused her more withdrawals. Next she took up the paper lists and this time began to read them more carefully. The one with symbols and abbreviations still made little sense, but the one with addresses made Cheryl feel suddenly self-conscious.

Her skin felt prickly, and the hair on her neck stood on end. She felt her heart pounding within her chest and knew that this had to be what the DEA so badly coveted. She licked her lips nervously and tried to decide what to do. From the sounds of it, the storm had died out or at least moved off in a direction away from the city. She looked at the first address and realized that she was quite familiar with the location. Getting there would be a breeze.

Getting there.

Since the shooting she'd not been out on her own even once. Now she was contemplating getting into the car and driving to a location where she had no idea what she'd come up against?

It couldn't be helped, she thought. She stuffed the list in her robe pocket and had started to replace the lockbox, when it dawned on her that she might need the keys. She reopened the lid and took out the keys as well. Replacing the box, she carefully used the toothpaste once again and secured the tile in place. Satisfied that it looked identical to the others, she hurried to get dressed.

It was only a little after seven when she pulled the car from the garage. She was relieved to find nearly a full tank of gas, and after one quick glance at the list, she mustered up her courage and pulled the car into the street.

Her nerves were stretched taut like radio-tower guy wires. Everything seemed to startle her. The traffic was heavy. She'd forgotten it was Monday morning. Rush hour began early in Denver, and this day was no exception. She maneuvered the car onto Interstate 25 and merged with the oncoming traffic. Beads of sweat formed on her brow, and her hands began to shake uncontrollably. Gripping the steering wheel tightly, she watched for her exit with an apprehensive eye.

Splash! A semi roared past her, spraying up water against her windshield. Cheryl let out a cry and swerved away, almost hitting the line of cars in the next lane. Fighting her fears, she steadied the wheel and signaled to move into the right-hand lane. Two more miles, she noted. Just two more miles and she would be at the appropriate exit. She tried to think about days gone by when she'd whip up and down the interstate like it was her own private drive. She'd been brave then. Brave and certain that nothing bad could ever happen to her. Well, that theory had certainly been blow apart.

She exited the freeway and made her way to the address on the list. The streets were waterlogged, and everything around her looked saturated from the early morning storm. The sky remained gray, lifeless, as though it couldn't decide if it wanted to rain again or not. She hated days like this. She always had. They seemed to drag on in indifference to everyone, not really threatening, but neither did they signal comfort. It was rather a harsh reminder of her own life. She was on permanent hold, or so it seemed. Neither living nor dead. Just existing.

She turned off the paved roads and found herself on a gravel road heading even farther south of town. The houses and businesses were fewer here, although there were still enough to give her a sense of security. She hadn't thought about anyone trying to harm her or approach her for an interview before leaving the house. What if some had followed her? Someone from the paper or television! They might try to photograph her.

She glanced around, checking her side and rearview mirrors. There didn't appear to be any ominous vehicle behind her, and no one seemed to give her the slightest attention as she drove past. *Good*, she thought and rested a bit easier.

Pulling up to a mailbox that marked a muddy drive, Cheryl noted that this was the first address on the list. A chain-link fence kept intruders from going any farther than pulling in off the street, and Cheryl decided to park and give the ring of keys a try.

Hesitantly, she got out and glanced around. No one seemed at all interested in what she was doing, and there didn't appear to be any other traffic on the road. She played at the padlock, trying first one key and then another, and had nearly given up when the mechanism released and the lock sprang open. Her mouth went dry. So far, so good. She swung the gate open and hurried back to the car.

Pulling down the muddy drive, Cheryl came face to face with a metal structure. It appeared to be some kind of storage building or small warehouse. Cheryl had the distinct feeling that she was about to unlock a great many secrets as she pulled the car around to the back. Wondering what she should do, she sat for several minutes in the silence of the morning. It would seem, she reasoned, that maybe Curt hadn't been so far out of line to believe that her father had played a much bigger role in the operation than anyone had imagined. After all, she was here, and the place looked deserted and seemed a very reasonable location for the exchange of drugs.

She got out of the car and walked around to the side of

the building where a single door and window were located. She tried the handle and found it locked. Remembering the keys she started back for the car just as she caught the sound of another car coming down the main gravel road. She froze. What if someone had followed her here? What if it were some of the drug people? She ran for her car and watched from its safety as the other vehicle passed down the road. It had slowed just enough to make Cheryl aware that whether they were there for her benefit or not, they were definitely interested in what was going on. As soon as they were well out of sight, Cheryl floored the gas, spinning mud everywhere as she made her escape.

Not even bothering to relock the fence gate, Cheryl hurried back into the city. Her heart was still racing when she made the street corner where her beauty salon was located. *Perhaps it wouldn't be wise to go home just yet,* she thought. *Maybe I should stop and talk to Michelle.*

Pulling into the parking lot, Cheryl suddenly realized it wasn't even nine o'clock yet. The salon wouldn't be open for at least two hours. Feeling rather foolish for her fears, she headed home and decided that she knew enough. She wasn't going to make any more amateur sleuthing trips. She hit the garage opener remote and pulled the car inside.

For several minutes she sat behind the wheel and forced herself to calm down. Whatever the list represented, there was no way she wanted it to fall into the hands of the DEA. It was hard enough to realize that her father had been involved with the drugs, but the list seemed to make it clear—that along with the money and fact that Curt had spoken of her father's confession. She'd never known Curt to lie, even when it caused someone else discomfort.

That, perhaps, was hardest thing of all to realize. Curt probably had every reason to suspect her father, and he was probably right about Grant as well. Suddenly she felt very alone, and the image of Erik Connors came to mind. She wished he were there to offer her his impish smile and soft-spoken words of comfort. Maybe she should call him.

"Maybe I will," she murmured. "There's no reason I shouldn't."

twelve

Erik wanted to sing all the way to Cheryl's house. She'd called him. She'd actually asked him to come to her house. Uncertain exactly what it meant, Erik tried hard not get his hopes up. It could be anything. She might want to tell him to stay away from her. On the other hand. . . He smiled. It could be that she was healing enough that she desired companionship.

He wheeled Ole Blue into the circular drive and shut off the engine. "Lord," he whispered before getting out of the truck, "please don't let me say the wrong thing. This looks like a good thing here, and maybe Cheryl's ready to accept that You really do care about her." He glanced at the house and felt a twinge of emotion as he continued. "Maybe she's ready to accept that I care about her, too." He sighed and opened the door. "Just don't let my feelings get in the way of helping her see that she can be forgiven. In Jesus' name, amen."

In the fading light, he noticed muddy tire tracks on the wet pavement of the driveway. It had drizzled rain off and on throughout the day, but not enough to wash away the evidence that someone had come to visit. Apprehensive, he wondered who was pestering Cheryl now. He ambled up the walkway and reached out to knock on the door, just as Cheryl opened it and greeted him.

"I'm glad you could come over," she said rather nervously.

Erik noticed that she was straining to look behind him, so

he too, turned to look around. "You expecting someone?" His heart took a bit of a nosedive, fearing that the only reason she had called was in order to have him strong-arm another unwanted visitor.

"No, just you," she admitted softly.

Erik turned back around and smiled. "Good. I like the sound of that."

She gave a shot at smiling and opened the door wider. "Come on in."

He followed her into the house just as the grandfather clock chimed seven. "So what did you do all day?"

"Nothing. At least nothing worth talking about," Cheryl said, directing them to the family room in the back of the house.

"I saw muddy tire tracks in the drive. Did you have visitors?"

Cheryl stopped abruptly. Her face seemed quite pale. "Ah, well, CJ stopped by for just a few minutes. She wanted to make sure I was okay after my last encounter with the DEA. She still hasn't managed to talk to Curt about it, but she intends to."

"What happened?" Erik asked, noting the agitation in her voice.

"It doesn't matter now," she said, waving him to take a seat. "Are you sure that you didn't already have plans for the evening?"

The evening? Erik wondered to himself. She'd said nothing about spending the evening with her. He decided to play it cool and not let on to how surprised he was by this turn of events. "No, I didn't have anything planned. I had to work overtime. You called just as I got home from the hospital. It was absolutely perfect timing."

"I tried calling earlier," she admitted. "I didn't know

what your schedule was."

"Well, it's fairly simple—at least usually it's fairly simple. I go to work at 5:30 in the morning. Actually my shift starts at 6:00, but I have to change into scrubs, so I need extra time. Then I work until 2:30, shower and change back into my street clothes, and home I go. Today was extra busy so they asked me to work over."

Cheryl nodded. "What all do you do at the hospital?"

Erik laughed. "It'd be easier to tell you what I don't do. Lab technicians hardly lead the glamorous life." He plopped down on the couch, hoping she'd do the same. When she did, he continued. "I draw blood from patients, and then I take it back to the lab and analyze it. Sometimes, the vampires do all the sticks, that is to say the lab assistants do all the blood collections." He grinned. "We have our own language at the lab."

"So you work with a microscope and decide what's wrong with people?"

"Sometimes, but a lot of times I run the blood through a series of machines. We have great computerized testing these days, and it's a wonder what you can learn about a person from blood. Your blood tells the story of your life." He thought of how this might make a great way to steer the conversation toward Christ, but before he could speak, Cheryl was asking him another question.

"Do you have a. . .well. . .someone in your life?" She lowered her gaze seeming quite shy about asking.

"You mean like a girlfriend?" She barely glance up and nodded. Erik shook his head. "No, there's no one at all."

"Why not?" she asked, seeming less embarrassed.

Erik tried to keep the conversation very casual. He didn't want to alarm her by bringing his new feelings for her into the picture. "I guess I just never found the right woman. For a long time I concentrated on school. I became a physical therapist before going back to college to become a lab tech. Everyone thought I was crazy because physical therapy pays a whole lot better, but I wanted to have a broad scope of training."

"Why's that?"

"I'd kind of like to go into missions work," he answered. He wondered what she'd think of this.

"You mean like to Africa or India?" She seemed horrified.

"No, probably more like South or Central America. There's a large number of destitute people down there, and they need a great many things. It also allows me to get in some extra flying time. That way I can keep up my license."

Cheryl rolled her eyes. "Another pilot."

Erik grinned. "Do you have a lot of us in your life?"

She seemed to grow sad. "Used to."

Erik didn't want to see her withdraw into the past, so he hurried forward with the conversation. "Anyway, enough about me. What about you? What are you going to do with yourself now that you've nearly recovered from the shooting?"

She shook her head and looked away. "I don't know. Daddy always figured I'd come into the business. O&F Aviation business, that is. I guess he figured I'd make a good ornamental executive or something like that."

"You didn't see it that way?"

"Not really. I'm not cut out for much. I don't have skills or schooling or training, and I certainly don't have the interest."

"What would you like to do? What are you good at?"

"Nothing," she answered flatly. "Nothing but causing trouble. . .apparently."

"I don't believe that for a minute," Erik said. "But I didn't come over here for a pity party." Cheryl's head snapped up at this. "I figure you have enough time by yourself to wallow in sorrow." He smiled. "Am I right?"

Reluctantly she nodded in agreement. "I didn't call you over for that reason either."

"Good. Why don't you tell me why you did call?"

"I just thought some company would be nice."

Erik thought she seemed to be hiding something, but he didn't push her. Maybe once she relaxed and realized he was willing to go the distance with her, she'd open up and trust him to understand her fears. "Do you want to go out?" he asked softly.

"No!" she exclaimed so quickly that Erik was certain something was wrong.

"Might I ask why?"

She looked at him, her blue eyes wide with fear. "I'm not ready for that."

"Okay. You want me to go rent some movies, maybe pick up some Chinese food again?"

"No!" She rubbed her arms as if chilled in spite of her long-sleeved blouse.

The desperation in her voice made Erik unable to remain silent. "Are you afraid of something in particular, or just everything in general?"

"It's just a bad day for me, okay? First the storm and then. . ." She fell silent.

"Then?" He reached out to touch her arm. "Then what?"

"Nothing. It's not important."

Erik was beginning to get a little frustrated. He wasn't about to sit around all evening trying to pull conversation out of Cheryl. On the other hand, he didn't want to hurt her feelings or to cause her more grief. He didn't know what do. Something was really bothering her, and he wanted to help. Then it dawned on him that maybe she'd changed her mind about having him over. Maybe she regretted it and just didn't know how to tell him to go.

"Do you want me to leave?"

"No! Why would you think that?" She seemed very upset with his question.

"I don't know. I guess because you're acting a bit strange. You're obviously upset about something, but you won't talk to me, and I thought maybe you were beginning to regret calling me over."

"Not at all." Cheryl let out a heavy sigh and seemed to search for words. "It's my father's birthday."

Erik relaxed. That explained a great deal. Of course she was having difficulty with the day. "Why didn't you just tell me that in the first place? I would have understood."

"I didn't want to be a baby about it all. It isn't the only thing that has me down, but it's one of the biggest reasons."

"So what do we do about it?"

Cheryl shrugged. "I'm not sure. Mary left some things to eat, and I could warm them up."

"That sounds good." He motioned to the television and video machine. "Do you have any movies you'd like to watch?"

"I don't know. We have a whole cabinet of movies over there," she said, pointing to a huge mahogany cabinet. "You could pick out something. Only. . ."

"Only?"

"Don't make it sad. I don't think I could take sad."

"Okay. You go fix us up something to eat, and I'll look for a non-sad movie."

Cheryl smiled weakly, and Erik noticed that for the first time since he'd seen her in the hospital, she was wearing the lightest touch of makeup. *She's pretty*, he thought. No, she was beautiful, and he knew that he was losing his heart to her. In spite of the fact that she'd warned him not to.

"Are you sure you don't mind staying?"

Erik wanted to go to her and pull her into his arms. He wanted to reassure her over and over that he didn't mind, but he was afraid that such a display of open emotion would send her running. So he played it as nonchalant as he possibly could. "I didn't have anything better to do."

She seemed satisfied with this and took herself off in the direction of the kitchen. After she'd gone, Erik let out his breath. His heart was pounding at ninety miles a minute. There was such a delicate balance to maintain, and he wasn't sure he could keep up his appearance of disinterest for much longer. He really like her, and he wanted to know her better—wanted to take her out and bring her into the world of the living. Knowing the kind of man Grant had been, he wanted to show her that some men were honorable and true. He wanted to prove to her that she could fall in love with a man and not get hurt.

And he wanted to be that man.

Walking over to the movie cabinet, Erik felt a burden on him like he'd never known before. This had started out as a holy mission, he reminded himself. He wasn't supposed to fall in love or have feelings other than those of a Christian brother for a lost soul. He opened the mahogany doors and stared in wonder at the vast selection of videos. There were old movies as well as new releases, and he had an endless supply of topics to choose from.

"Don't make it sad," she had said, and he could still see the pleading in her sapphire-blue eyes.

"Nothing sad," he said, running a finger over each of the listed features.

He tried desperately to remember the plots and incidents of each and every movie. A love story might upset her because of what she'd lost. A movie with children, especially babies, might depress her because of the miscarriage. He reached for one, then remembered it had a shooting scene and by-passed it for the obvious reasons.

Comedy! That's what we need. We need something funny. Something slap-stick and nonthreatening. His fingers had just touched a tape marked "Three Stooges Marathon" when Cheryl's blood-curdling scream tore through the silence.

Erik thought his heart had stopped. He rushed to the kitchen and found her trembling as she pointed to the window with one hand and covered her mouth with the other.

"What was it?" he asked, rushing to the window. He looked out into the darkness, but saw nothing.

"I saw. . ."

"What? What did you see?"

She shook her head. "I thought I saw someone out there. I thought I saw my father."

Erik turned away from the window and went to her. He wrapped her in his arms as he had wanted to do from the first moment he'd stepped foot in the house. "It's okay. Sometimes that happens when you lose someone you love."

"I think I'm going crazy," she sobbed and gripped his upper arms as if to steady herself.

"You aren't going crazy, Cheryl. It's a natural process of mourning. A lot of people think they see loved ones after they've died. It's just that we want so much for them to be alive that our mind plays tricks on us."

"See, I told you I was going crazy. My mind isn't working right anymore."

Erik pulled her tighter. "That's not true. Hey, I thought I

saw Candy after she'd died."

"You did?" Cheryl looked up at him as if seeking the truth of the matter in his eyes.

"Yes. It happened one morning when I was walking into the intensive care unit at the hospital. See, that's the last place I saw her alive, and it must have just stuck in my mind. Anyway, I was talking to this one nurse, and I looked down the hall and there she was. I was so shocked I had to look away, and when I looked back, I could see that it was just another nurse. It wasn't Candy at all, but in my heart I guess I wished it could have been. I really wanted her to be alive and well."

Cheryl nodded. "Sometimes I wake up hearing a baby crying. I thought maybe it meant I was crazy. I don't want to be crazy, Erik." She put her head on his shoulder and said nothing more.

For several minutes they held each other. Erik wanted to give her strength and peace, but at the moment, he wasn't sure how much he had to share. She'd managed to shake him up in a way that he couldn't explain or ignore. If he said much more, he was certain that he'd declare his love for her. And he couldn't do that. Not yet. Not when she was so vulnerable to the past.

He stroked her hair, breathing in the scent of what could only be described as a garden of wildflowers. He liked the way her curls slipped like silk through his fingers and the way her head seemed to fit just right against his neck. He wanted the moment to go on forever.

Suddenly Cheryl pulled back. "Stay with me tonight," she pleaded.

Erik said nothing, but he knew his expression relayed his surprise.

"I don't mean anything by it," she continued, in a tone

of desperation. "Not in a sexual sort of way or anything like that. I'm not like that. . .not really. I just can't stand another night alone in this house."

Erik regained control and shook his head. "I know you aren't like that," he whispered. He saw gratitude in her eyes as she realized he meant every word. "But I can't stay here with you."

Her expression fell. "Why not? Are you afraid of what people will think because of me?"

He shook his head. He couldn't tell her the truth, it might drive her away from him for good. "No, I'm not afraid of what people will think. It's just that I know it wouldn't be good for either one of us. But I have an idea."

She looked at him warily. "What?"

"Why don't you stay the night with CJ? I know you two are good friends, and I know from what she told Curt and Christy that she'd wanted you to come recuperate at her house anyway."

"I'd hate to impose," Cheryl said, barely whispering the words.

"I don't believe for one minute that CJ would find it an imposition. Why don't I call and make the arrangements while you go upstairs and pack what you need?"

"I just don't know."

"It'll be the best thing. You'll see. Staying with CJ will keep you out of the public eye and give you a time of peace and quiet while someone else worries about the details."

"I guess we can try, but what if she says no?"

He thought her very much like a little child who needed desperately to know that the monsters in the closet wouldn't get her. "She won't say no. She loves you," he answered. *I think I love you, too.*

"I guess that would be okay."

"Great. Now you go get your things, and I'll call CJ."

He watched her reluctantly leave. She seemed to war within herself about the decision. He went to telephone and then realized he didn't know CJ and Brad's number. Dialing directory assistance, he memorized the number they gave, then hung up the phone and redialed.

"Hello?" a sweet feminine voice sounded.

"CJ? It's Erik Connors."

"Hi, Erik. What's up?"

"I'm at Cheryl's and wondered if I could ask you a favor."

"Sure. What is it?"

"Well, Cheryl's a little upset. She thought she saw her father outside the window, you know, just her mind playing tricks and what not. I figured, given the fact that today's his birthday, it's probably extra hard on her." When CJ said nothing, Erik continued. "Anyway, I wondered if she could come spend a couple days with you. She's at the point where she doesn't want to be alone, and I think it would be a good idea if we rallied round her and made sure that she didn't have to be alone."

"Of course she can come. Brad and I will be right down."

"No, that isn't necessary. I'll bring her up. I think I remember the way. Look, I really appreciate this. She seems so scared, and even before she thought she saw Ben, she was obviously agitated and upset about something."

"Did she tell you about her encounter with the DEA?"

"She mentioned it, but wouldn't go into detail. What happened?"

"Why don't I tell you when you get here. I'm certain it has more to do with her fears than anything else right now."

"Why do you say that?" Erik asked, suddenly sensing that CJ was keeping something from him.

"Because," CJ replied, "today isn't Ben's birthday. His

birthday is sometime around Christmas."

"I see what you mean. Okay, well, I'll have her out there shortly."

"Erik?" CJ called to him. "Don't be mad at her for lying. If I were going through half of what she's been through, I'd probably try to cover up my feelings too."

"I'm not mad," Erik answered. "Just disappointed. I wish she'd learn that she can trust me."

"Apparently, if she's letting you bring her to me, she's already learned that lesson. Just give her time. I think she's greatly embarrassed by what she's done in the past, and how it's taking it's toll now is anybody's guess."

"I suppose you're right." Erik bolstered his courage once again. "I'll see you soon."

He hung up the phone and looked back at the window for a moment. If today wasn't her father's birthday, maybe it was no ghostly apparition she'd seen at the window. Maybe someone was stalking her for information or for some other reason. He had just determined to go outside and check for footprints when Cheryl reappeared, travel bag in hand.

"I'm ready," she whispered.

Erik forced aside his doubts and worries. "Great. Tell you what. We'll stop for fast food on the way. How's that sound?"

Cheryl gave him a tight smile. "Sounds fine."

thirteen

Cheryl felt a sense of peace wash over her as CJ and Brad's three-story, native-stone home came into view. She'd remained awkwardly silent throughout the ride, wondering whether she should play it straight with Erik and explain about the list. He'd already proven himself loyal to her in their friendship, but he was Curt's brother-in-law, and she couldn't take the chance that he might even accidentally tell the DEA about the list.

"Are you still okay with this?" Erik asked, pulling into CJ's drive and parking the truck.

"Yes, I think so." She tried hard not to think about how much she'd come to trust him. Would she tell him too much? Would she give too much of herself to him? She pushed these fears aside and reached for the door handle. "Thank you for bringing me out here."

"Hey, I'm not running off until I know for sure that you feel comfortable. I even told CJ that I planned to come in with you."

Cheryl smiled. Once again he'd put her comfort in front of his own. He could be spending the evening out with friends or relaxing at home after a hard day's work. Instead he was chauffeuring her and making sure she was safe and happy.

They walked in silence up to the door where CJ stood waiting for them. "I've watched for you for about the last ten minutes."

"We'd have been here sooner, but I had to feed her,"

Erik offered good-naturedly. "She can't cook, you know."

Cheryl looked up and shrugged. "I suppose there's no sense in defending myself. Everybody here knows that's true."

CJ laughed. "I was never much of a cook either, but Brad is so demanding. . ."

"Hey, did I hear my name mentioned?" Brad questioned, striding into the foyer.

"Hi, Brad," Erik said, pushing Cheryl forward. "CJ was just telling us how you forced her to learn to cook."

Brad put his arm around CJ's shoulder and hugged her close. "Yes, well, if she'd been any less proficient with airplanes, I probably wouldn't have married her at all."

CJ elbowed him sharply, while Cheryl and Erik exchanged a smile. Cheryl knew the truth of this love match. She'd been with CJ when Brad had first come into her life. "Did you ever hear the story of how they met?" Cheryl surprised them all by asking Erik.

"No, I can't say that I have."

"Well, before you get started on that old story," CJ said, "why don't you come in and make yourselves comfortable."

"Sounds good to me," Erik said and followed Brad's example by putting his arm around Cheryl. "Lead the way."

If anyone was surprised by his actions, no one said anything, and Cheryl relaxed, allowing him to take her to a plush gold-colored sofa. He sat down, almost in unison with her and seemed not the least bit hesitant about remaining close at her side. Cheryl thought at first that his nearness would make her feel awkward, but instead it had just the opposite effect and she turned to him with an enthusiasm she'd not felt in months.

"CJ used to be quite claustrophobic, and she got herself

locked into the bathroom of one of Brad's hotel rooms. I went for help and thought Brad was one of the hotel maintenance people."

"She nearly pulled my arm out of its socket to get me upstairs with her," Brad commented.

"Well, after he got her out of that bathroom, he didn't have to be forced to remain at her side," Cheryl added.

"Yes, but that was only after I'd thrown up and totally humiliated myself in front of him," CJ said with a laugh. "You know it has to be true love when a man forms a relationship with a woman after he's held her head over the toilet."

They laughed, and Cheryl felt a certain comfort that she'd so long missed in her life. She felt safe here and knew that no one would come to hunt her down and demand answers that she couldn't give. There was always the possibility that Curt would show up to see CJ, but Cheryl knew that CJ would protect her.

"Let me get us something to drink," Brad offered. "We have all kinds of soda, iced tea, juice—so what'll it be?"

Erik looked at Cheryl. "Tea sounds great for me," Cheryl said, trying hard not to notice how blue Erik's eyes were.

"Make it two," Erik told Brad. "You need any help?"

"No, you go ahead and visit. This will only take a second."

CJ lost little time in striking up the conversation. "Cheryl, Erik said you were feeling pretty spooked this evening. Are you feeling better now?"

Cheryl nodded. It was easy to remember her earlier discomfort, but in this house she knew it was far from her. "It was kind of a hard day," she said. Then remembering that she'd told Erik it was her father's birthday, Cheryl had a pang of conscience. "I lied to you, Erik," she said, suddenly needing to confess the truth. "Today isn't Dad's birthday."

Erik exchanged a quick glance with CJ before asking, "What was it then?"

Cheryl took a deep breath. "It was a lot of little things. Everything just catching up with me I guess. Ever since that Damon Brooks guy tried to break my wrists, I just haven't been the same."

"Damon Brooks? Who is he, and why didn't you say something about his trying to hurt you?" Erik asked, extremely agitated by this news.

"He was the DEA agent who came over the other day when CJ was there. I wasn't sure I wanted to talk about it," Cheryl admitted. "I suppose I have to accept that this kind of thing is just going to be my lot."

"They have no right to hurt you. What happened?" He looked first to Cheryl and then to CJ.

CJ took a seat just as Brad returned with the drinks. "Well, this guy showed up as I was leaving, and Cheryl asked me to stay while he questioned her."

"Thank goodness I did," Cheryl said softly.

"No, thank God you did," CJ corrected. "I think God divinely oversaw that entire episode. If I hadn't been there, there's no telling what he might have done."

Erik was now very upset. "Just what *did* he do?"

"He got really ugly with Cheryl, demanding that she produce a list of her father's contacts and drug drop-off locations. It was the same information Curt had already asked her about, but Mr. Brooks certainly didn't use Curt's manner." CJ took a glass of iced tea from her husband before continuing. "He pushed Cheryl around and finally grabbed her by the wrists and yanked her up off the sofa. He twisted her arms so that she was in a lot of pain."

Cheryl pushed up the sleeves of her lightweight cotton blouse. Her wrists were encircled with bruises, and Erik's normally jovial expression, turned markedly angry. "Why didn't you tell me earlier about this?"

Cheryl shrugged. "What could you have done?"

"I know what I intend to do," Erik replied, gently touching her wrist. "I'm going to Curt on this. I'm surprised you haven't already talked to him, CJ."

"I've tried," CJ admitted. "But he hasn't been around, and I didn't want to talk to Christy about it. Plus, it didn't seem like the kind of thing I could discuss with just anybody down at the DEA office."

"Well, I'll get ahold of him. There's no call for this kind of thing."

Erik was gently massaging her wrist, and Cheryl very nearly lost all thought of her earlier concerns. His touch was mesmerizing. What was happening to her?

"Well, someone definitely needs to get to the bottom of it," CJ said without trying to camouflage her own anger. "I was terrified. He threatened to break her arms when I started to call the DEA."

"What kept him from doing it, anyway?" Erik asked.

"Mary showed up," Cheryl answered. "I guess he figured three women were too many to deal with."

"It's uncalled for, and I wish I'd been there to keep it from happening."

He let go of her, and Cheryl almost wished she could brazenly bring his hand back to hers. But she didn't. She steadied her nerves and took a long drink of the tea. Everyone was upset because of what had happened to her. The tension in the room made her uncomfortable. She'd come here for her own peace of mind, and now it seemed that she'd caused problems for everyone else. It suddenly seemed necessary to apologize for her part in their discomfort.

"Look, I want to say something, and I'm not exactly sure how to begin," she finally spoke.

She drew another deep breath and tried to start again. "I loved my father a great deal, and I don't want to think badly of him. Still, I know there are things I probably ignored and problems I never knew about. I don't want Dad's memory put through the mill, grinding it up into grubby little bits, all the good along with the bad. He wasn't really as bad as some people want to make him out, but I guess I'm ready to admit he was no saint." She held up her hand when CJ started to speak. "I guess love overlooks a lot of mistakes."

"That's what the Bible says," Erik interjected.

"Well, then," Cheryl said, considering this for a moment, "you can see where it's true. Anyway, I guess what I want to say is that I'm sorry for the way each of you have been dragged into this. CJ, you know I loved your mom and dad. They were like an extra set of parents, and they were fun loving and kind, and I'll always mourn their passing."

CJ wiped tears from her eyes, and Brad moved in to sit on the edge of her chair and put an arm around her. Cheryl felt a twinge of jealousy that constricted her speaking for a moment. CJ had found true love—love in such a rare and pure form. Cheryl looked away quickly, afraid that her expression would betray her own longing.

"And Erik, I know I've been particularly hard on you. You've offered me nothing but human kindness and encouragement. I'm really sorry that your sister suffered because of me. . ." Her words trailed off. She didn't know what else to say. She was able to admit that she was sorry that she'd ever met Grant Burks, but not to this crowd. They hated him enough, and to add to that seemed like it would be throwing gasoline on a fire already out of control.

"You can't blame yourself, Cheryl," CJ said. "You were

deceived. We all understand that."

"Curt doesn't. He thinks I'm knee-deep into whatever Grant and Dad had going on. And frankly, I still don't believe that Dad knew everything that was happening."

"He probably didn't," Brad agreed.

"But whether he did or not," CJ continued, "you have to understand that we don't hold you accountable for something your father did or didn't do, for that matter. As for Grant, well, you are no different than hundreds, no thousands, of other women who fall for men who woo and wow them, only to use them for information and material benefit. Grant was good at what he did."

"And I was very much in need of being loved," Cheryl said softly.

"You were just naive," CJ added.

"Well, I don't intend to ever be that naive again. I'm through worrying about being loved."

"Don't give up on love," CJ said, looking up at her husband with such an expression of contentment that Cheryl felt like running away. "It'll come at you when you least expect it."

"I can vouch for that," Brad said, laughing. "Maybe you should develop a good case of claustrophobia."

Cheryl had to smile. "Those bathroom doors in your hotel still sticking?"

They all laughed, and Cheryl felt the acceptance that she so longed for. Maybe her healing was finally beginning. Maybe CJ and Erik had been right. Maybe harboring bitterness and anger kept a body from healing.

"Look, I'm going to have to get back," Erik said, glancing at his watch. "I have to be to work quite early."

"Well, don't worry about a thing," CJ assured him. "Cheryl will be fine here, and she can stay as long as she wants to."

"Good. I'll rest easy knowing she won't have anymore encounters with the DEA. I intend to talk to Curt first chance I get."

He got up, and without thinking, Cheryl followed him to the door. With CJ and Brad awaiting her in the other room, she felt compelled to express her thanks once again. "Erik, I just want you to know that I appreciate what you did for me tonight. I don't know when any of this will be over, but I appreciate your friendship, in spite of what I might have said in the beginning."

Erik's impish smile returned, and without warning, he leaned down and kissed her cheek. "Well, maybe someday you'll be ready for something more than friendship."

At that he turned and left. She touched her hand to her cheek and stared after him in stunned silence. He knew all her secrets. He knew about Grant, and the baby, and her father, and still he suggested the possibility of something more than friendship.

Cheryl closed the door as soon as Erik fired up the truck. She leaned against the wall and marveled that anyone could know the truth about her and still care. God cared, too, Erik had told her. Dared she believe it, too, might be true?

Later that night, Cheryl lay awake in CJ's guest room. She thought a lot about how CJ and Brad had welcomed her with open arms. *They love me*, she thought, and instantly she knew beyond a shadow of a doubt that it was true. CJ cared for her. After all they'd come through together. After the desertions and reunions and conflicts and resolutions, CJ still cared for and loved Cheryl as much or more than she had when they were children.

"It's me," Cheryl whispered to herself. "I'm the one who rejected her love. I'm the one who put Erik at arm's length." She thought of Erik and his parting words. Cheryl knew from experience exactly what he'd meant by those words. She might be naive when it came to giving her heart to the wrong man, but she knew the possibilities of what Erik had in mind.

Maybe someday you'll be ready for something more than friendship. His words hung in the air as though he'd just spoken them.

Cheryl thought of the past and what she'd done and how far she'd strayed from what she knew to be right. "I've disappointed so many people," she said sadly. "But most of all, I've disappointed myself. I've been stupid and very foolish. Now I have a chance to make it all right, and what do I do? I run away. I leave Curt needing vital information—information which I have. I put everyone's life in danger, and I selfishly cower behind the protection of the only friend I've ever really known."

The silence of the night weighed heavy on her. She couldn't deny the truth anymore. She needed to go home and retrieve the papers for Curt. She needed to swallow her pride, admit her mistakes, and go on from there. *Grant is dead. Dad is dead.* And no amount of mourning would bring them back, nor would it make them into the people she had believed them to be.

Rolling onto her side, Cheryl began to formulate a plan. Her future depended on coming to terms with the past. And her past could only be concluded when she turned over all the evidence of her father's involvement with the drug ring.

fourteen

Erik knew he wouldn't be able to concentrate on anything until he'd spoken to Curt about Cheryl's encounter with the DEA, and yet he had his obligation to the hospital. All through the day, however, he barely kept his mind on work, and it wasn't until he'd nearly thrown out the wrong specimens that his supervisor pulled him aside.

"You got a problem, Erik?"

"Look, Joe, I'm sorry. I've got some family troubles, and I guess my mind is just a wee bit preoccupied."

"Just a wee bit," Joe said with a laugh. "Look, why don't you clear out of here?" He glanced at his watch. "There's less than two hours left on the shift, and who knows what kind of damage you could do in that time?"

"It's okay, I'll stay. I mean, I'm off tomorrow and the next day anyway."

"No, I insist. You're making me a nervous wreck. Now go shower and get out of here."

Erik didn't argue further. He knew he wouldn't relax until he had some answers from Curt. It worried him that Cheryl would continue to be subjected to DEA strong-arm tactics, and if he had even the remotest chance of protecting her from such a thing, Erik was ready to go to battle for her.

He arrived at Curt and Christy's around one-thirty in the afternoon, and to his pleasant surprise he found Curt's car in the drive, while Christy's was nowhere to be seen. With any luck at all, he'd have Curt to himself and not have to explain to his big sister what was going on. Ringing the bell, he was greeted by a stern-faced Curt.

"We need to talk. It's very important." Erik paused before adding, "It's about Cheryl."

"Okay," Curt said, sounding rather hesitant.

"Are we alone?" Erik questioned, glancing around as Curt led them to the kitchen.

Curt threw his suit coat onto a chair in the hall before replying. "Yeah, matter of fact, I was just stopping in for lunch. You want something?"

"No. I'd rather get this off my chest first." Erik couldn't help remembering how angry he'd made Curt when he'd interfered with his investigation. Would he see this as yet another interference? What if Curt thought the DEA had handled things exactly right? Feeling a frustration born of anxiety, Erik blurted out the first thing on his mind. "I don't like the way your people are treating Cheryl."

Curt had just opened the refrigerator and turned to stare blankly at Erik. "What are you talking about now?"

"Look, I took Cheryl out to spend some time with CJ. She was so upset and spooked that she thought she'd seen someone at the kitchen window last night."

"And had she?"

Erik shrugged. "I don't know. I was going to go outside and check, but she didn't seem to want me to leave her. At first she lied and told me it was her father's birthday. Later at CJ's, she came clean and told me it was just everything getting to her, including the DEA's rather ugly visit a few days ago."

"I don't have any idea what you're talking about," Curt said and returned to the refrigerator to rummage around for his lunch. "Why don't you sit down and tell me everything from the beginning? I'm just going to make a sandwich. You want one?"

"No." Erik tried to explain what he knew about Damon Brooks' visit. It seemed an inadequate portrayal of what had taken place, but since he hadn't been there to witness the situation himself, he tried to stick to the facts supplied him by CJ and Cheryl. Curt brought his sandwich and drink to the table and ate in silence as Erik continued.

"So when CJ said that he'd threatened to break Cheryl's arms if CJ called you at the DEA office, I figured enough was enough. You guys have no right to treat her like that. Her wrists are black and blue!"

Curt stared back with a dumbfounded look on his face. "I didn't know anything about this. When did you say this took place?"

"I'm not sure. Several days ago," Erik offered, trying to remember if CJ or Cheryl had indicated an exact date.

"And the man's name again?"

"Damon Brooks. Do you know him?"

Curt shook his head. "I've never heard of him. But that doesn't necessarily mean anything. Look," he glanced at his watch and got up, "I'm going to call in to the office and see what's going on. We'll get to the bottom of this."

Erik sat back and waited for what seemed an eternity. He was naturally concerned about keeping Cheryl safe, but he was also quite unnaturally overwhelmed with the feelings he had that went far beyond concern for her safekeeping. When had he come to care so much about her? Had it been in the hospital when she'd lingered between life and death and Erik had wondered if Grant Burks would claim yet another life? Maybe he'd really fallen in love with her when she'd pleaded with him to take her away from Curt. It was impossible to say, but what counted was that Erik knew now, more than ever, that he had fallen in love with Cheryl Fairchild.

Erik could hear Curt in the other room. His voice was lowered, but the anger came across nevertheless. He caught bits and pieces of the one-sided protest.

". . .should have been consulted. . ."

". . .my investigation. . ."

Then Curt's voice raised. "Look, do we have a Damon Brooks or not?"

Silence followed, and Erik found himself growing more and more uncomfortable. The only real peace he had in this situation was knowing that Cheryl was safely with CJ and Brad. He didn't like to think of her at the Fairchild house with no one around to protect her. Of course, she had a security system, but it wasn't foolproof. If someone wanted to get to her, they'd have little difficulty in doing just that.

He heard Curt slam down the receiver and stomp off down the hall. Erik got to his feet and came out into the hallway, just as Curt returned, strapping on his shoulder holster and gun.

"What's going on?"

"The DEA has never employed a man named Damon Brooks. They didn't send anyone out to speak with Cheryl." He eyed Erik quite seriously. "That means someone else wants the same information we are after. And the only other people who know that such a list exists and who would have any need for it—"

"Are the drug traffickers!" Erik interjected.

"Exactly."

"Tell me more about this Damon Brooks," Curt demanded.

"I don't know anything more than I've already told you," Erik answered honestly. "But CJ and Cheryl could tell you everything. Why don't you call your sister?"

Curt nodded and reached for the telephone. "I'll do that." He dialed the number, talking to Erik the whole time. "If it was one of the drug people, we need to put some round-the-clock protection on Cheryl." He waved Erik's reply into silence. "CJ, it's Curt."

Pause. "I'm okay, but I need to talk to Cheryl."

Erik waited anxiously while Curt listened to CJ. "So how long ago was that?" Curt asked. "Okay. Did she say why?"

What is she saying? Erik wondered.

"Okay, CJ. I'll reach her there." Curt replaced the telephone receiver and turned to Erik. "She says that she took Cheryl home a couple hours ago. It seems Cheryl had something important to do. Something that involved giving me a call."

"Do you suppose she found the information you had asked for?"

"I think she's probably always had it," Curt replied. He ran his hands through his hair and sighed. "I just wish I could have convinced her to give it to me a long time ago. We could have avoided a great many problems if she had."

"But maybe she doesn't have it at all. Maybe she just wants to talk to you about the investigation and let you look around the house."

"There's no way of knowing unless I ask her. I'm going to give her a call." He picked up the receiver again. "Hopefully we can get to the bottom of this in short order and I can find out who Damon Brooks is."

Erik gave Curt Cheryl's new unlisted number, and waited anxiously as Curt punched in the number. After a long pause, Curt hung up.

"No answer," he said in frustration.

"That's strange," Erik said. "She always leaves the

machine on to pick up the calls."

"I'm going over there." Curt grabbed his suit coat and put it on, hiding his holster and gun.

"I'm going too," Erik said, giving Curt a fixed and determined stare. "And you aren't going to stop me."

"Look, Erik—"

"No, you look. I've come to care more about her—more than I should, perhaps—and I'm not going to bow out of this gracefully. She's in trouble, and I want to be there for her. Maybe she has the information you need, maybe not, but either way, I intend to be there for her."

Curt considered his words before nodding. "Fair enough, but you do things my way."

"I owe you that much," Erik replied, already heading for the front door.

They made their way to the driveway where Erik started to get into Curt's car. "You follow me," Curt said. "I think it's better that way."

Erik did as he was told, even though he had little desire to be set off on his own. He feared that somehow Curt would keep him from following or that through some strange twist of fate, Ole Blue would fail him and he'd never make it to Cheryl's house. But none of his fears came true. Blue started as smoothly as ever, and Curt drove at a steady pace in order to allow Erik to keep up with him.

At Cheryl's house, there was no response to Curt's pounding knock, nor to his multiple rings of the doorbell. The entire place was as quiet as a cemetery, and Erik began to feel fear gnaw holes in his resolve.

Curt went to one of the living-room windows and stared through the tiny opening where the drapes didn't quite meet. "It's too dark to see inside," he told Erik and went back to the door. He tried to force it open, but to no avail.

"I'll go around back," Erik offered.

"I'll come with you."

Together they made their way around the side of the house, checking along the way for the footsteps Erik had wondered about. "If there was someone here," he suggested, "he would have made tracks right over there." He pointed beneath the kitchen windows, and Curt made his way over to check the grass.

"It looks pretty trampled," Curt said, kneeling down. "I'd say there was something more substantial than ghostly images out here last night."

Erik shuddered. "Glad I took her to CJ's."

Curt nodded and got back up. "I just wish she'd stayed there." He went to the back door and tried it, but it, too, was lock. He tried to look through the door's curtained window, but again he was thwarted. "I don't suppose she gave you a key?" he asked Erik.

"No, we aren't exactly that close. Not yet."

Curt raised an eyebrow but said nothing. Instead he studied the back door. Then, without a word of warning, he took up a small yard statuette and bashed in the back door window.

The sound of glass breaking made Erik's blood run cold. It haunted him in a way that he couldn't explain. He watched as Curt reached a hand inside and unlocked the door, and still he couldn't explain his apprehension. What if they were too late? What if the person who had watched Cheryl last night had returned?

Curt pulled his gun, and Erik felt his mouth go dry. "What is it? Did you hear something?"

"No, it's what I'm not hearing that makes me wary."

Erik frowned. "I don't understand."

"There ought to be all kinds of alarms going off," Curt replied, cautiously moving into the house. "Ben had this place wired to the max. Someone has obviously disabled the system."

Erik followed his brother-in-law into the house. Immediately, he could see that the place had been torn apart. Dishes and pans had been pulled from the cupboards, and cans of food and box mixes were strewn about the floor.

"I'll wager the rest of the house looks the same," Curt said, moving toward the kitchen door. "Why don't you stay here?"

"Not on your life," Erik replied. "She might need me."

Curt nodded and motioned him back. "Then stay down and far enough behind me so that I can maneuver."

They moved out into the hallway and found the house ransacked just as Curt had figured. Nothing had been left untouched. The cushions of the couch and chairs had been cut apart. Even the drapery linings had been cut away from the drapes. Erik felt a tightness in his chest and throat. Where was Cheryl when all of this was going on? Where was she now? Would they find her upstairs, dead?

As if reading Erik's mind, Curt spoke. "She might have found this mess when CJ dropped her off. Maybe she high-tailed it out of here and went back to CJ's."

They moved together up the stairs. Erik felt the tension mount. He'd like to believe that Cheryl was safely with Curt's sister, but it didn't seem likely. He felt bad. Very, very bad. His stomach hurt, and his breathing came so rapidly that he was certain he'd soon be hyperventilating. Forcing himself to breathe more slowly, he let his gaze travel over the ravages of the intruder's attack. In the bedrooms, the mattresses had been cut up and searched, while the drawers and closets had been emptied and clothes had been left precariously around the room.

"They were very thorough," Curt commented, and after searching out all of the upstairs rooms, he holstered his gun and turned to Erik. "My guess, however, is that Cheryl had whatever they wanted hidden away. Apparently they never found it, and my guess is that Cheryl interrupted their search."

Curt went to the telephone, then shook his head and motioned Erik to follow him. He went outside the same way they'd entered, then went to his car to use his cellular phone.

"CJ, it's Curt again. Look, did Cheryl come back to your place?" Pause. "No, she's not at her house. I'm here with Erik, and the place has been torn apart."

Erik waited helplessly as Curt calmed his sister. "Look, we'll find her, but if she shows up there, make sure she stays put and gives me a call. Okay?" He pressed the disconnect button and instantly redialed. He looked at Erik while waiting for the call to go through. "I'm bringing in help. This one's bigger than we can handle alone."

Erik nodded, and he knew by the grave expression on Curt's face that he suspected the worst.

"It's O'Sullivan. Look, get a team over to the Fairchild house. The place has been ransacked and Ms. Fairchild is, at this point, missing. My guess is that she's been taken hostage."

Erik felt as though Curt had dealt him a blow below the belt. He sucked in air and tried to force his lungs to accept the offering, but his head was spinning from the realization that they were too late. He hadn't been able to save her from harm, and now she might well be dead.

Leaning back against his truck for support, Erik's only

recourse was to offer up a prayer. "Oh, God," he whispered, as Curt continued to talk with his people, "please keep her safe from harm. Don't let them hurt her. Please God, don't let her be dead."

fifteen

Cheryl's hip ached from the brutal way she'd been thrown into the back of the utility van. Ropes bound her hands behind her and prevented her from steadying herself as the van bounced mercilessly through a series of twists and turns.

Her mind blurred with images of the house being destroyed by the two thugs who now held her captive. Tears filled her eyes as she thought of all her treasures being broken to shards. So many years of memories now lay in ruin, and the thought of her loss was the only thing that drew her mind from her current predicament.

They'd wanted the contents of the lockbox. At least she knew from their demands that they wanted the list and the keys. No mention was made of the money, so perhaps the money had belonged solely to her father. She'd lied and told the men she had no idea where such a list might be. They'd slapped her, knocking her off her feet, so rather than fight, Cheryl had remained complaisantly seated on the floor until their curiosity had been satisfied.

Now, in the darkness of the van, Cheryl choked back a sob and bolstered her resolve not to cry. *I won't give them the satisfaction of seeing me fall apart*, she determined. Yet even as she thought this, fear gripped her body and held it as captive as the men who'd placed her in the van.

She tried to focus on Erik, forcing herself to remember his face. She outlined in her mind his sandy-colored hair and blue eyes. She mentally drew a picture of his impish grin and the way his face always suggested an inner joy and happiness. He said it was the peace of God acting in his heart. He had said on more than one occasion that the joy God gave him just bubbled out from the center of his being and flooded everything in its path. Cheryl couldn't imagine having that kind of joy.

Oh, Erik, where are you now? Why didn't I listen to you and stay with CJ?

But she already knew the answer to that question. She'd returned to the house with every intention of calling Curt and turning over the list that she'd safely replaced in the lockbox before going to CJ's. Instead, she found herself taken hostage by two rather nasty-looking characters, and reconciling the past with Curt was instantly made impossible.

Remembering Curt and how she'd treated him, Cheryl found herself wishing she could at least set the record straight before dying. She didn't really hate him anymore. The pieces of the puzzle had slowly come together, and in spite of her desire to believe her loved ones free of guilt, the truth was hard to ignore. She could now accept that Grant had brought this trouble down around him. Little things popped into memory. Things that had transpired between her and Grant. Things that had seemed odd at the time but Cheryl had chosen to ignore in hopes that they were mere coincidence.

But neither coincidence nor chance had landed her in the back of this van on the way to an unknown destination. Struggling to sit up, Cheryl found herself unable to make out any detail of her surroundings. The van's cargo hold was completely separated from the driver's position. There wasn't a single shred of light to give her even a hint of an image. She struggled against the ropes which bound her hands. They were too well tied to work loose, and each movement only managed to cause her more discomfort.

The van turned sharply, and Cheryl barely managed to balance herself by throwing her right leg out to the side. She came in contact with something metallic and maneuvered her leg across the top in order to get a better idea of what it might be. It seemed to be some sort of toolbox. The cool metal surface was evident even to her jean-clad leg, and in the center, a handle of some sort disturbed the smooth lines of the box.

She brought her right leg back and gingerly put out her left leg in the opposite direction. A soft mound of material easily gave way to her prodding limb before her foot made contact with the van wall. The van moved from the paved road to one of gravel. Instantly Cheryl lost her balance and fell back against the floor. She could hear the gravel striking the undercarriage of the van and felt as though her teeth would be jarred right out of her head by the sudden roughness of the road. *Where are they taking me?*

The van seemed to slow, and Cheryl felt her heartbeat pick up speed. Her mind began to race with thoughts of how she would handle herself. Could she talk her way out of the situation? Could she plot out a method by which she could dupe her captors? *There has to be an answer*, she thought. *After all, I still have the list and the keys.* She smiled to herself in the darkness. Maybe they were her trump card in all of this. Maybe she could face her captors with the same aloof toughness she'd given most everyone else for the past five months. *It might work.*

The van launched itself down an even rougher road, and Cheryl moaned painfully as her head slammed against the metal floor again and again. She struggled back into a sitting position but found this only marginally better. The ride seemed endless, and what little hope she'd managed to bolster within her heart died out when the van finally came to a screeching halt and slammed her against the cold steel walls.

This is it, she thought and waited for someone to open the doors to the cargo area. But they never came. They left her alone and went off arguing between themselves. She heard the voices fade into the distance, and a sinking feeling came over her.

What if they never intended to give her a chance to come up with the materials? What if they were only bringing her out to some deserted place in order to kill her? Cheryl began to panic. She fought against the ropes with a vigor born of desperation. It was useless.

Cheryl began to pray. Fear and hopelessness made it seem the only thing left to do.

"God, I know I'm a mess. I know I don't deserve any kind of consideration on this," she began, "but I need a way out. I need help." She swallowed hard, trying to keep her voice steady and her thoughts centered. "CJ and Erik have both tried to help me see the need for having You in my life, but until this moment I guess I figured I was quite capable of taking care of myself." She lowered her voice to a whisper. "Guess I was wrong."

Cheryl tried to remember what it was CJ had said about salvation. What was it she was suppose to do in order to be forgiven? Surely there was more to it than being sorry and asking for God's mercy. It couldn't be that clear-cut. Could it?

"God, I don't know all the right words," Cheryl admitted. "I am sorry for what I've done, and I certainly don't intend to do anything like it in the future. Is that enough? Is being sorry and determined never to do wrong again enough to have Your forgiveness?"

Her heart was in turmoil. What if God couldn't forgive her? What if the things she'd done were too bad to be forgiven of? But CJ and Erik had both said that God loved her and that He wanted her to find the truth. *What truth?* Cheryl wondered. Maybe it was the truth of her own stupidity. If that were the case, she'd already learned that lesson.

Find the truth.

She pondered that for a moment. She remembered a verse from the Bible that spoke of the truth setting you free. Could the truth set her free now?

"God, I just don't know what to do. I'm sorry for my life, and I ask you to forgive me. I want to be saved from this mess." Then she remember CJ speaking of God's salvation. Salvation from Satan's deceptions. Salvation from self-destruction. Salvation from eternal death.

"Yes, that's it," she murmured. "I want to be saved. I want you to save me, God. If I'm not too bad to save, then show me. Show me by saving me out of this physical mess and then I'll know that You are able to save me from my spiritual mess as well."

For reasons beyond her understanding, Cheryl felt comforted. It wasn't as if the doors had magically opened or her bonds had instantly fallen away. But a small portion of her anxiety had lifted, and in that, she found an understanding of peace. It wasn't an emotional thing, because God knew her emotions were well out of control. The thought almost hit her as a settled matter. God not only could save her. He would save her.

Voices sounded outside the van, and Cheryl braced herself for what was to come. Could she hold onto that tiny slip of faith? The doors opened, and Cheryl blinked rapidly against the light of day.

"Come on," the larger of the two men said and gave her legs a yank. He dragged her to the end of the cargo area and pulled her out by the shoulders. "The boss is ready to see you."

Cheryl faced the man as bravely as she could. "Who is he, and why does he want to see me?"

Offering no explanation, the man grabbed her tightly around the upper arm and pushed her forward. The smaller of the two men glanced around nervously, and Cheryl followed his gaze. They were leading her toward a metal building. It looked like an old airplane hangar with two large doors slid back to leave the interior exposed. Looking beyond the building, Cheryl could see nothing but open space. She realized they were facing east. The mountains had to be behind her, and she tried to twist enough to look over her shoulders to assure herself of this fact.

"Stop gawking around," her captor told her and roughly pushed her forward.

Cheryl would have fallen except for the man's continued hold. She tried to think of where they might be. There were several old airfields in the area, but which one was this one? Could it belong to O&F Aviation? She tried to find some shred of evidence that might confirm or deny the possibility.

"I told you to knock it off," the man said, growling out his displeasure. "It ain't gonna do you any good, anyhow."

Cheryl remained silent as they passed inside the hangar. She looked around and saw nothing but old oil drums, crates, and filthy workbenches. She'd focused on a rusted-out sign, when the man who held her, pushed her forward and this time released his hold. She fell to the oil-stained cement and found as she tried to get back to her feet, that another man had joined them.

"Help her up," a deep, husky voice commanded.

Both men took hold of her and brought her back to her feet. Cheryl steadied herself before allowing her eyes to meet the face of the man who controlled her captors. With a gasp, she felt the strength drain from her body, and once again, she sank to her knees.

Looking up again, still unwilling to believe what she was seeing, Cheryl found the man's amused expression. His dark complexion and dark eyes might have made him a handsome man in his younger days, but a thick ugly scar marred the left side of his face. That feature alone kept him from being an older version of Grant Burks.

&

"I'm telling you everything I can think of," Erik said impatiently.

"I'm sorry, Erik," Curt said. "It's just that any detail might help us in figuring out what's happened."

Erik nodded. "I know that, and I want more than anything to help you get Cheryl back, safe and sound. It's just that I don't know what's helpful and what's not. I can tell you that there were what seemed hundreds of telephone calls daily. That's why she changed her number. Some of them were legitimate enough, but Cheryl did mention that a great many calls were from people who claimed to be friends of the family and clearly weren't."

"Did she have any idea who the people really were?"

Erik tried to ignore the DEA agents working around him. It was distracting to see strangers going through Cheryl's personal belongings, but he knew it was necessary. "Not really. I think she felt pretty certain that a lot of them were reporters wanting information on the drug situation and her father. When she had her number changed, the calls stopped."

"What about last night? Did she say what she saw outside the window?"

Erik shook his head. "She only said that she'd thought she'd seen her father. But honestly Curt, I think she only said that to throw me off. She didn't want to admit at that point that she was upset about anything other than her father's death and the fact that she missed him."

Curt ran a hand through his hair. "Okay, start from the beginning. Why did you come over in the first place?"

"She called me. It was the first time she'd ever invited me over. She seemed pretty agitated, you know, kind of nervous and uptight." Curt nodded, and Erik continued. "Anyway, when I got here, she opened the door and seemed pretty glad to see me. She was looking around like maybe she was expecting someone else, and I even asked her about it."

"What did she say?"

"Only that there wasn't anybody else coming."

"Is there anything else that sticks out as unusual?" Curt questioned, his voice edged with desperation.

Erik started to shake his head, but then stopped. "I do remember asking her about the muddy tire tracks in her drive. Remember it rained early yesterday morning? Anyway, there were these muddy tracks in the drive, and I asked her where they'd come from."

"What'd she say?"

"Only that CJ had stopped by to check up on her."

"But that isn't true," Curt said, suddenly seeming very interested in the matter. "I just talked to CJ to get the details on that Damon Brooks character, and she said she'd not seen Cheryl since that incident. She'd only talked to her on the telephone."

"Then the tracks belonged to someone else," Erik said flatly.

"Exactly where were they positioned?"

"Right in front of the garage."

"Debbie, come here for a minute," Curt called to an exotic-looking young woman.

Erik smiled as the woman approached. She was dressed smartly in a navy blue suit, with her black hair swept fashionably into a French twist. Erik recognized her as one of Curt's DEA partners. She had been the one working with Curt when he'd first met Christy.

"What is it, Curt?"

"I want you to go to the garage and check the vehicles there for any signs of mud or recent usage."

"Sure thing."

She took off, and Erik looked back at Curt. "What are you thinking?"

Curt shrugged. "Maybe nothing. Maybe everything. What if Cheryl, herself, made those muddy tracks?"

"But Cheryl hadn't left the house since coming home from the hospital. Well," Erik paused feeling rather embarrassed to bring up his mistake of the past, "except for the time she went with me."

"But what if she did leave the house? What if she went in search of something or someone?"

"But who or what? I know how upset she was about facing the public. It would have had to be something big in order to make her leave."

Debbie returned just then. "There's dried mud all over the tires of the green Volvo."

"That's Cheryl's car," Curt said flatly. "She must have gone somewhere."

"I can take a sample of the dirt and try to analyze where it came from," Debbie suggested.

"She couldn't have gone all that far," Curt murmured,

obviously thinking through the situation. "It would have had to be sometime either during or after the storm because everything was pretty dry up until then."

"And as scared as she was of everything," Erik offered. "I doubt she would have driven anywhere very far out of Denver."

"I'll get a sample and see what I can turn up. Maybe it will give us something to go on."

"Thanks, Deb," Curt replied, still deep in thought. "Someone figured out that Cheryl knew about the list. There's evidence of that just in the fact that Damon Brooks or whoever he was came to question her about it. What if Cheryl knew where the list was and tried to do some exploring on her own?"

"To what purpose?" Erik asked, seeing immediately the direction Curt's thoughts were taking.

"Clearing her father," he answered flatly. "It's the only thing I know that she would have felt strongly enough about to put aside her own fears and leave the house."

"But even if she had the list, chances are she doesn't have it now," Erik reminded him.

. Curt shook his head. "I don't think that's necessarily true." He looked around the room as if seeing it for the first time. "Either they got what wanted and Cheryl surprised them and they felt they had to take her with them to keep her quiet, or they didn't find what they wanted and they took Cheryl with them to force her to help them."

"Either way, it doesn't look good for her," Erik commented grimly. Things were definitely not shaping up the way he'd hoped they would.

sixteen

"My name is Severon Burks," the man told Cheryl. He maintained a regal bearing and an attitude of aristocratic disinterest. "As you may have already surmised, I am Grant's father."

Cheryl nodded, knowing beyond any doubt that the man was speaking the truth. Looking into his eyes was like looking into the ghostly image of the man she'd once loved.

"Why am I here?"

He smiled tolerantly and motioned to the two thugs. "Bring a chair and some rope. Ms. Fairchild looks a bit spent."

"I'm fine," Cheryl protested, not wanting to be any further confined than she already was.

Burks ignored her and waited until the men had tied her securely to the chair before continuing. "My son was a bit remiss in his duties. There is a list of information that I need to complete certain business transactions. I believe you have that list, and I want it now."

"I don't know what you're talking about," Cheryl replied, meeting his eyes. She knew she had to make this convincing. "For the last five months, people have nagged me to death about a list, and I'm going to tell you the same thing I've told everyone else. I don't know about any list." She drew a deep breath and held it, hoping that her trembling wouldn't be so noticeable.

"You aren't a very convincing liar," Burks said, brushing

bits of lint off his otherwise immaculate black suit coat. His jaw appeared to tighten, and his eyes narrowed in a menacing way. "You don't seem to understand how this game is played." He leaned down until his face was only inches from her own. "I don't care what happens to you. Dead or alive, I will have my information."

Cheryl thought of the lockbox securely hidden in her bathroom. It gave her a sense of control to know that it wouldn't be easily discovered. Surely if she maintained her calm, collected appearance and held her ground, Grant's father would have to let her go.

Severon eyed her suspiciously for several moments. "I knew that Grant had lost his mind when he deemed it necessary to involve himself with you. I warned him about the complications, and now he's dead. You're to blame for that. You and that Curtiss O'Sullivan character. Do you suppose I would stop at anything to get back what is mine?"

Cheryl felt a shudder tear through her and tried to cover it by coughing and twisting in the chair. "I don't have anything that belongs to you. I don't know what list you're talking about and. . ." She paused, trying to muster her courage. "I'm not to blame for Grant's stupidity."

Severon seemed taken aback by this, so Cheryl pushed her point home. "You let my father's reputation be ruined and all because of some father-and-son drug business. Why do you suppose I would help you even if I could? I made the mistake of falling in love with your son. It doesn't mean I'm inclined to make further mistakes by aiding the enemy."

Severon snapped his fingers, and one of the men who'd taken her hostage appeared with a small suitcase. The man held the case flat while Burks undid the clasps and opened the lid. He thrust the man forward until the case was clearly level with Cheryl's eyes.

"This is why I know you are lying."

Cheryl looked at the rows of neatly wrapped one hundred dollar bills. "I don't understand," she said flatly and forced herself to look at Burks.

He motioned the man away. "My men retrieved this money from the warehouse you so easily led us to yesterday morning. The warehouse was only one of a great many exchange locations on your list and had you not gotten spooked, no doubt you would have led us to other locations."

True panic gripped Cheryl. She had to think fast. She had to offer up some logical reason for going to the warehouse. "I still don't know what you're talking about. The warehouse was property owned by my father. I thought perhaps he used it for storage, and since I'm in the process of trying to settle his affairs, I went there to see what might be housed inside."

Burks shook his head. "No, you didn't."

Cheryl could see that he didn't believe her. His rigidly fixed features frightened her to the core of her being, but there was absolutely nothing she could do. To tell him about the list would mean her certain death, and suddenly Cheryl didn't feel so inclined to give up her life. She tried to muster up anger in order to counter her terror. There had to be some way to fight this. *Please God*, she prayed, *give me some way out*.

"I'm growing impatient with you, Ms. Fairchild. We both know that the list exists, and we both know that you have the list, as well as the keys that go to each of the locations on that list. I expect for you to turn both over to me, and I'm going to tell you exactly how it's going to be handled."

Cheryl tried hard to face her adversary without emotion.

"By all means, please tell me how I'm to perform this magic feat for you."

Burks gave her a leering grin, and it was so like the ones Grant used to offer that Cheryl felt her blood run cold. What had seemed attractive on Grant now struck her as hateful and evil.

"You are going to make a telephone call," he said simply. "You are going to call my son's killer and tell him where he can find the list and the keys and have him bring them here to me."

"You. . .want me. . .to call Curt?" she asked hesitantly.

He crossed his arms and nodded very slowly. "Oh, yes indeed. I intend not only to reclaim what is mine, but also to avenge the death of my child. You see, it really doesn't matter to me that the operation has been compromised. There are other operations and other ways to bring cocaine into the U.S. It was great using O&F Aviation while it worked, but nothing is foolproof, and in this case, the fool is one Curt O'Sullivan."

"He'll never come here just because I call," Cheryl said, trying to think her way out of the situation. "He hates me now. I blamed him for Grant's death and for the death of our unborn child." She paused to see what kind of effect her statement might have on Burks. His expression never changed. "He won't come to my rescue if that's what you'd hoped for."

"He'll come."

"I'm telling you—"

"He'll come," Burks said angrily. "He'll come because of his need to clear his father's name. After all, isn't that what has driven *you*?" She couldn't hide her surprise, and this made Burks laugh. "You aren't dealing with a simpleton, Ms. Fairchild. I've been in this business for the past twenty years, and frankly, I've gotten quite good at it. Now, you'll make the call, and you'll be very convincing. You'll instruct Mr. O'Sullivan as to where he can retrieve the goods, and then we'll relay the directions to this hangar."

Cheryl knew time was running out, yet still she protested. "I can't help you."

Without warning, Burks yanked her head back and put a gun to her throat. "You will either make the call, or I'll kill you and make the call myself. It really doesn't matter. I'd prefer to watch O'Sullivan suffer as he watches you die, but either way, I'll have my list. You see, that list represents millions of dollars of hidden drugs and laundered money. You aren't going to convince me with your sugary sweet innocence, and you aren't going to rob me of the pleasure of seeing you and your murderous friend die."

He pressed the barrel of the gun harder against her throat. "I'm going to give you a countdown. If you don't agree to make the call by the time I get to 'one,' then I'll blow your head off and resolve the matter without you."

Cheryl swallowed hard and felt the gun press even tighter against her windpipe.

"Five. . .four. . ."

What could she do? What should she do? She didn't want to die, but neither did she want to be responsible for Curt's death.

"Three. . ."

But she was afraid, and her fear won out.

"Two. . ."

"All right. I'll make the call," she whispered, barely able to force the words from her mouth.

Severon smiled and pocketed the gun. He released her hair and ran his fingers lightly down the side of her face. "I knew you come to see things my way."

Erik followed Curt into his house, determined to convince him to let him somehow help find Cheryl.

"You don't understand," Erik protested as his sister joined them.

Christy's face betrayed her confusion, and Curt instantly sought her help. "You have to convince your brother that I know what I'm doing and that he doesn't. He needs to stay out of my business."

Christy looked first to Curt and then to Erik for some further explanation. "You aren't making any sense," she said. "Convince him of what?"

Erik shook his head before Curt could explain. "Don't bother to tell me that it isn't my business. I'm in love with her."

Christy's eyes widened at this, and Curt threw up his arms dramatically. "If you love her, then let the professionals take care of the situation."

"What is going on!" Christy suddenly demanded.

"Cheryl Fairchild has been taken hostage. At least we think she has. If not, then she's on the run from someone," Curt finally offered.

"And *he*," Erik said, waving an arm at Curt, "doesn't understand why I want to help find her."

"I didn't say that I didn't understand it. I simply said that you aren't qualified to throw yourself into the middle of a DEA sting operation."

Christy paled. "Erik, he's right. You have to stay out of whatever Curt is doing. I know from experience that it can only lead to innocent people being killed or hurt."

"That's why I want to help. Cheryl's life is in danger, and whether you think she deserves saving or not, I love her and intend to help her."

Christy exchanged a glance with Curt. "You love Cheryl?"

Erik's shoulders sagged, and he let out a heavy sigh. "Yes. I've fallen in love with Cheryl Fairchild. So before you go into some kind of lecture about her history and the fact that she's not good enough for me or whatever else you might conjure up, keep in mind that we all make mistakes. Even you."

Christy nodded. "I wasn't going to lecture you. I'm just surprised."

"Why, because you don't think she deserves love?"

"Stop taking the defensive with me, Erik. I don't like the part she played in Candy's misery, but I'm willing to let the past go," Christy said, sounding rather angry. "Furthermore, I remember my own mistakes very well, and I'd be the last one to say that Cheryl can't be forgiven for the past. I would question, however, whether she wants to be forgiven of the past."

"I think she does. I think she's only just come to realize how much harm she's done herself in believing in people who didn't deserve her devotion. She let herself be used and manipulated. You know how that feels, Chris," Erik said, remembering a time when Christy had fallen prey to a deceptive college professor. The man had tried unsuccessfully to press Christy into an intimate relationship, and he might have succeeded had Christy not found out that he was married.

Christy's expression softened, and Curt put his arm around her rather protectively. "I remember very well how it feels," Christy said. "Feelings aren't what matters here, however." She looked at her husband and gave him the briefest of smiles. "You can't jeopardize Cheryl or yourself by sticking your nose into a situation that's way out of your league. Would you want Curt coming into the lab and telling you how to run things there?"

Erik felt totally defeated. "Of course not. But you don't understand." His heart ached with the thought of what Cheryl might be going through. "She's out there somewhere, and she's alone."

"She's not alone, Erik," Curt said, his voice taking on the first real hint of compassion. "God's watching over her, and we have to pray and trust Him to take care of her in this. She can't be held accountable for the sins of her father, but those sins have obviously revisited themselves upon her. We can't wish her out of this, and you can't go running wild in hopes of locating her. You can, however, stay here and pray. And not only for her, but also for me and my team."

Christy reached out to touch Erik's arm. "He's right. You know he is."

"I suppose so."

Just then the telephone rang, and all eyes turned in unison as if anticipating what the call would reveal. Curt left Christy's side and went to answer it.

"Hello."

There was a long pause. Erik watched Curt's face for some sign of the news, but the only thing he noted for sure was the way his brother-in-law's face had grown pale.

"I understand. Are you okay?"

Now Erik was certain the caller had to be Cheryl. He moved toward the phone, but Curt held out his hand to ward him off.

"Do what you're told. I'll be there as soon as I can." Curt hung up the telephone and turned to face Christy and Erik.

"It was Cheryl, wasn't it?" Erik asked, almost fearful of the answer.

"Yes."

"Is she. . .was she. . ."

"She's being held just outside of town. She told me where the list is, and I'm to bring it to her captors."

"I'm going with you."

"You can't, Erik," Curt said quite seriously. "And if you fight me on this, I'll have you arrested."

"But I love her."

"Yes, and they'll kill her if they see anyone but me."

Christy moved away from the men and sat down hard on a nearby chair. Erik noted her frightened expression. It seemed to match his own fear.

"Do *you* have to take it to them?" she asked weakly.

"I was specifically named," Curt replied.

He didn't say anything more. He didn't have to. Erik knew beyond all doubt that such a declaration meant only one thing. Someone had a grudge against Curt and intended to resolve the matter by having him deliver the goods.

"I could stay out of sight. You know, hide in the back of the car or even the trunk," Erik offered.

"No."

"But Curt, you can't just walk into a trap."

"I know what I'm doing, Erik." He looked at his wife and then at Erik and added, "I need you to watch out for Christy. She's going to need you more than I will."

Erik could see that he was right, but he didn't want to give in. Cheryl needed him too, and he longed to be the knight in shining armor that she could depend on.

As if sensing Erik's inner battle, Curt spoke once again. "You can come to Cheryl's house with me and help me retrieve the list. But after that, I want you to come back here and stay with Christy. Will you do that for me?"

Erik drew a deep breath and nodded. There was no other choice.

☙

They found the Fairchild estate swarming with DEA agents when they arrived. Curt immediately led the way upstairs to Cheryl's bathroom and began throwing shampoo and conditioner off the ledge that lined the bathtub.

Debbie called to them from the doorway. "Frank passed along your cellular-call message. I've got everything set up here."

"Good. Thanks, Deb," Curt said, prying the toothpaste caulking away from the tile. "Cheryl is one smart girl. I can't believe she dreamed this up on her own. It's brilliant. Who would ever have thought to look here?"

"Obviously no one did," Erik said, leaning back against the vanity, while Curt stood in the tub.

The tile snapped off and Curt quickly cast it to one side. He pulled a penlight from his pocket and flashed it into the dark hole. "Bingo!" He reached his hand inside. "Well, it's a tight fit. . .but I think. . ." He fell silent and pulled the lockbox from the hole. "I've got it!"

Debbie leaned her head around the door. "Is that it?"

"Yes," Curt said with a certainty that Erik envied. "She said everything we needed was inside." He scrambled out of the bathtub and put the box on the vanity. "Let's see what we have." He tried to release the clasp, but it stuck. Taking out a ballpoint pen, he maneuvered it between the lid and the box and finally managed to pry the thing loose.

"Wow!" Erik exclaimed at the sight of the thousand dollar bills. "That's some piggy bank."

"Tag it," Curt said, handing it to Debbie. "These too." He put the diskettes into her hands. "Well, here's the cause of all our troubles." He held up the keys in one hand and the papers in the other.

Erik considered the objects for a moment, then grimaced.

The cold, hard reality of what was actually happening had finally begun to sink in. "They're going to kill her, aren't they?"

Curt met his stare and shook his head. "Not if I can help it."

"But maybe you can't. Maybe she's already dead."

"Thinking like that won't help anything," Curt said sympathetically. "You have to trust God on this one, Erik. Illegal activities and concealing evidence is what stirred this into a real hornets' nest, and it won't be easily resolved. But with God, well, I believe we're on the side of right and truth. God will honor that, and I trust Him to watch over us in the process."

"But Cheryl is alienated from God," Erik said sadly. "I wasn't able to convince her of His love for her."

"Don't be so sure," Curt said quite seriously.

"Why do you say that?" Erik looked to his brother-in-law for a hope that might carry him through this nightmare.

"Because she told me she was sorry," Curt answered softly. "She told me she was wrong."

"I hope that's enough."

"I feel confident that it is. Now listen to me, Erik. The DEA isn't going to take this thing lightly. We have the full cooperation of the Denver police, and together, they'll have all the possibilities figured out before I even go in there. You have to help Christy stay calm. She needs to be there for Sarah, and you need to be there for her. You know how she worries, and you know how stubborn she can be. Please go back to the house and wait for me there. When it's all over, I'll come there first."

"And Cheryl?"

Curt grinned in his cocky self-assured way. "I'll bring her with me."

Erik wanted to believe him. "Would you do me one favor?"

Curt sobered. "If I can."

"Tell her that I love her. You know, just in case—"

Curt's smile was back in place. "You don't have much faith in me, do you?" He turned to leave. Calling over his should he said, "You tell her yourself when we get back."

Erik wanted to run after him and demand to be allowed to go with him, but he knew it was no good. Going after Curt would only put him in danger. Sneaking around behind his back might even get Curt and Cheryl both killed. Fighting the urge to handle things on his own, Erik sat down hard on the edge of the tub. For the first time since Candy's death, he felt like breaking into tears.

"It isn't manly to cry," he could remember his father saying without the slightest regard for his son's pain.

It might not be manly, Erik said to himself, *but it certainly is human.* He sat there for several minutes before deciding there was nothing more to be done.

Walking through the house, he ignored the tight gathering of agents as they listened to Curt. Outside, the light was fading from the sky as the sun melted into a puddle of orange and gold behind the Rocky Mountains. Erik climbed into Ole Blue, feeling so lost and discomforted that he didn't know what to do. Where was God in all of this?

"I'm with you always," an inner voice seemed to speak.

Erik pounded the steering wheel with his fists. "But I need assurance. I need to know that she'll be okay."

Calming a bit, Erik fell back against the seat and shook his head. "God, I know You care, and I know You have everything under control, but I'm afraid. I don't want anything bad to happen to Cheryl. I don't even know where she is, but you do. She's alone and scared, and I just want You to stay with her."

Then surprisingly the words of a Psalm came to mind, and Erik murmured them aloud. "Where can I go from your Spirit? Where can I flee from your presence? If I go up to the heavens you are there; if I make my bed in the depths you are there, If I rise on the wings of the dawn, if I settle on the far side of the sea, even there your hand will guide me, your right hand will hold me fast."

Erik breathed a sigh of relief and felt a peace wash over him that he'd not believed possible under the circumstances. God wouldn't desert them. He wouldn't desert Cheryl. Even in the depths of this hideous situation, God was there.

"I have to keep my focus," Erik said and started the truck. "I have to remember that God loves Cheryl even more than I do.

seventeen

Cheryl gagged at the taste of the oily rag in her mouth. Severon didn't want her screaming to warn Curt away, yet he wanted Curt to clearly see that Cheryl's life depended upon his actions. Therefore, Burks left her tied and gagged in the middle of the hangar with both doors open and a single light shining from nearby. As shadows fell across the ground and the skies darkened, Cheryl felt desperation build within her soul.

I'm the bait they're using to capture Curt, she thought. *I'm the reason he's going to die.*

She tried not to think about it. She tried not to think of how she and Curt had come full circle. She'd loved him once. She had planned her life around a future that would see him as her husband and lifetime mate. Those memories were bittersweet. The Curt and Cheryl of those yesteryears no longer existed. Yet the affection had been very real.

But she had hated him as well.

Someone had once told her that love and hate were opposite sides of a single coin. She didn't know if she believed that or not, but in analyzing her hatred, Cheryl found that such feelings were far more internalized than she'd originally believed. Instead of hating Curt, she found that she really hated herself. Hated her vulnerability. Hated her neediness. Hated her mistakes. Hating Curt for injustices, real or imagined, came easy. Already steeped in hatred, Cheryl had little ability to love anyone.

But now Curt would face death because of her hatred

and her love. It was all her fault, and now all she wanted to do was protect him. She thought of Christy and of Grant's baby. *What was her name? Oh, yes, Sarah.*

They loved Curt and needed him. How could she ever explain that her stupidity and stubborn refusal to assist Curt had cost them a husband and father? Tears welled in her eyes as she watched and waited for the telltale signs of car headlights.

Then another face came to mind. Erik. She tried to concentrate on her memories of him. His boyish grins. His blue eyes, so bold and bright. He could gaze at her with a look that seemed to go right through to her soul. Just thinking of him caused her stomach to do a flip.

I suppose, she admitted, *that since I'm about to die it can't possibly hurt anything to say I've come to care for him.* She wanted to laugh at her own noncommittal thoughts.

Care for him? The man who'd forced himself into her life and beaten down the walls of hatred she'd built? The man who bore her painful reminders of the past? The man who knew all her dirty little secrets and held no condemnation for her?

She pulled restlessly at the rope that bound her to the chair. Erik was also the man who'd comforted her when she was afraid. He'd been the man who'd refused to be put off, the one who'd gone the distance with her and remained true to her needs.

Maybe someday you'll be ready for something more than friendship. His words came back to haunt her.

I am ready for something more, she agonized. Only now, there might not be a "someday" to count on. She might never have a chance to tell Erik that she'd fallen in love with him.

I've fallen in love with him? she questioned. Her heart knew that it was true. It wasn't the teenage love she'd had for Curt: a love born out of familiarity and adolescent vision. It wasn't the adventurous emotion she'd felt with Grant. No, this was a quiet, saturating kind of love. The kind of love a woman knew she could count on for the rest of her life. The kind of love that would see her through the thick and thin of things and come through stronger than ever.

Headlights flashed before her eyes, and Cheryl instantly forgot her thoughts. Curt had come, and no doubt with him came her only hope for surviving Severon's revenge. She tried to glance around to where she'd seen Severon take his hiding place. The darkness prevented her from seeing him there, however. She looked overhead where the two thugs were calmly waiting in the shadows, no doubt with guns drawn.

If there were only some way to save Curt's life! Cheryl knew she would offer herself up in his place. He didn't deserve to die for this. He'd only been after the truth. And with that thought, Cheryl knew that she could completely forgive Curt for the imagined wrongs she'd held against him.

Curt's car stopped just outside of the hangar. She could see him now. His expression was quite serious, and for several moments all he did was look at her.

Don't come in here, she thought, and then she prayed, *God, don't let him be killed.*

Curt got out of the car slowly. In his right hand he held the lockbox. Raising both hands aloft, he moved toward her with an ease that made Cheryl want to scream. She struggled against the ropes and made as much protesting noise as her gag would allow. Curt only smiled and winked at her with a cocky self-assurance that made Cheryl want to slug him. This was life and death. Didn't he understand the jeopardy?

If we die now, Cheryl thought, *then everything has been in vain. Daddy will have died in vain. The O'Sullivans' deaths will mean nothing. Even my baby's death will be forgotten and meaningless in the wake of Severon Burks' victory.*

Curt advanced, and Cheryl could see his eyes dart from side to side, even though his face remained fixed on her. "I'm here, Cheryl. I've done exactly as you instructed me."

She moaned against the rag, wishing that he would magically disappear from the line of fire. She suddenly remembered in vivid detail the way it felt to have a bullet pierce her body. At first it had just been a stunning sensation of being hit hard in a very small space. Then it had seemed a warmth spread through her body until it became a white-hot fire. Her breath caught in her throat, and her chest tightened. She shook her head, refusing to allow the memory to take her captive. If there was even the remotest possibility that she could help Curt, then she had to stay clearheaded and focused.

"I've brought your precious list," Curt announced to the air. "So why don't you stop playing this game of hide and seek and come out and inspect it for yourself."

"I believe I'll do just that," came the voice of Severon Burks. He stepped into the light, gun leveled at Curt's midsection. "I suppose introductions are unnecessary."

"I know very well who you are," Curt said, slowly lowering his hands. "Severon Burks, age fifty-eight, Columbian born to a native mother and American father. Raised in Columbia until the age of twelve, when your mother died and your father relocated to the U.S. in order to see you receive an American education. You stayed on after the death of your father, married, and raised a son named Grant. When Grant turned eight, you moved your family back to Columbia and joined your mother's family in the cocaine business."

"You've done your homework, Mr. O'Sullivan."

"Just as I'm sure," Curt said with a smile, "you've done yours."

Severon smiled. "You're quite right, of course. We probably know each other better than we know ourselves."

"I don't know that I would go that far, but I suppose we're knowledgeable enough to respect the deadliness of our opponents."

"Exactly."

Cheryl watched the showdown with growing agitation. She couldn't move. She couldn't speak. She could hardly breathe.

"I've brought what you want, now why don't you let Ms. Fairchild go so we can get down to business?"

"Not so fast." Severon waved the gun at Curt and motioned toward a small workbench. "Put it over there, and then go stand beside her."

Curt toyed with the lid's handle. "I would imagine you'd like to review the contents and make certain this is what you've been waiting for. After all, I could have an empty box here, and then you would be back at square one. Wouldn't you like to see?" He looked up with a questioning expression.

"You wouldn't be stupid enough to remove—" Brooks fell silent, and his eyes narrowed.

Cheryl drew in a sharp breath, and Severon stepped toward Curt. "Yes, I suppose you would be stupid enough to believe that removing the contents would buy yourself more time."

Curt shrugged and gave the man a good-natured smile. He rolled his head back just a bit and gazed upward as though considering the nature of their conversation. Cheryl watched him and suddenly realized that Curt was studying the surroundings. He was looking for something or. . . someone!

Would Severon notice? She began to make noise, hoping that if he did, he'd forget about it and focus on her.

He looked at her with an unyielding expression of anger. "Be silent." He waved the gun in her direction. "Or I'll silence you myself."

Cheryl cowered down against the back of the chair and nodded. *It was enough*, she thought. Curt had been able to give the area a good once-over. *At least I've helped that much.*

"All right, Mr. O'Sullivan. On the chance that you think you can mastermind some form of heroics in this matter, I'll review the contents of the lockbox first. I will add, however, that if the box contains less than I expect it to contain, I'll put a bullet through the kneecap of your friend over there. You can watch her suffer in pain while we figure out what to do about your inability to follow directions."

"I didn't say that I'd neglected to bring what you asked for," Curt responded quite seriously. "You're just like your son. Grant also had a penchant for using women to buffer himself from harm. Why don't you stop hiding behind Cheryl's presence and look it over? I want to get home, and I want this matter to be settled. You win. You have your list, and you have your drugs. That should make you a very happy man."

"It might, but you neglect to remember one simple fact." Severon's expression turned to a look of pure hatred. The scar on his face grew tight and pale. "You killed my son.

That isn't something I'm going to forgive you for. You're going to pay for what you've done, and she can pay as well."

"I didn't kill Grant," Curt replied frankly. "Forensics proved that much. My bullet didn't kill him. I was busy getting his fiancée out of the line of fire. My only concern at that moment was to keep my friend from dying."

Cheryl blinked back tears. He had risked his life for her. It was a simple fact she had been quite willing to forget, yet here was history repeating itself.

"You're to blame for the double-cross. That makes you responsible for his death."

Curt shrugged. "Have it your way, but Grant brought it all on himself. He didn't even stop at endangering the life of his child. Sarah was just another pawn in this stupid game of yours."

"The child is of no concern to me. Put the box down and move over there." Severon was clearly through playing games. "You people operate under the delusion that your own principles for living can somehow be grafted onto those around you. My game is different from yours, and its rules are different. Life is short and fleeting—and in most cases very fragile. It isn't the life of a person that matters quite as much as what can be accomplished with that life."

"Then why avenge your son's death?" questioned Curt. "If life is of so little value, why spend your time and energy here?"

"Because several million dollars are at stake," Severon replied. "And because I am a businessman. When you take something of mine, you must pay for it. You took the life of my son, and I will take yours." He raised the gun. "Now, put the box down."

Cheryl wanted to scream. Curt came to stand beside her,

yet his presence did nothing to comfort her. Even when he put his arm on her trembling shoulder, Cheryl found her body tensing even further.

Severon smiled at them with an evil leer that made Cheryl draw in a sharp breath. Would he kill them now?

"You may have already seen my friends overhead," Severon said as he put his own gun into his suit-coat pocket. "I wouldn't try anything foolish. They've been instructed to shoot you both if you so much as sneeze."

"Good thing I don't have a cold," Curt said snidely.

Severon stared hard at him for a moment, then turned to the box. He fumbled with it for several minutes before growling in anger and turning back to face Curt. "It's stuck."

"Yeah, it does that. I find that a ballpoint pen usually does the trick. I have one right here, if you need it. See, you just pry it between the lid and the box—"

"Then get over here and do it, and remember my men have you and your friend covered. One wrong move will see her dead."

"Relax, Severon. Your friends at the gate have already made certain I'm not carrying any weapons. They went over the car in detail, and they did everything but strip-search me. How could I possibly pose a threat?"

How indeed? Cheryl wondered, yet she prayed that Curt might be just such a threat. She wanted nothing more than for Curt to find a way to release them both from the clutches of Grant's father. Sitting there, helpless, she thought of every movie she'd ever seen, remembering the hapless victims and how they staged their own rescues. But this wasn't a movie. She had no carefully concealed knife in her shirtsleeves. She had no prearranged plan for an army of mercenaries to storm the premises and whisk her and Curt to safety by the sudden appearance of a blimp or fully-armed jet. Her only hope was that God had listened to her prayers.

Curt walked to where Severon stood and reached slowly into his breast pocket. Cheryl tensed. She could tell by the look of concentration on Curt's face that he was about to make his move. She'd seen that look a hundred times before. *What can I do to help? What can I do?*

Suddenly it seemed important to distract Severon's concentration. Cheryl began to strain at the ropes and rock the chair in place. She yelled from behind the gag, calling Severon every name she could think of—all of it coming out in garbled, incoherent groans.

It was enough, however, to make Severon turn. Just as he turned, Cheryl rocked the chair too hard and it went smashing against the concrete floor. Lying perfectly still, Cheryl feared that the men overhead would riddle her body with bullets. She could almost feel the impact of the bullets piercing her flesh. It was that nightmarish day of the DEA shoot-out all over again.

She heard the scuffle between Severon and Curt, but was unable to see the results. Overhead she could hear voices and shouted commands. There seemed to be a great deal of yelling and confusion. What in the world was happening?

Everything went silent. She tried to raise her head up enough to see, but it was impossible, so she waited silently for her fate.

"I've got your boss," Curt shouted to the rafters. "If any of you wants to play hero, now's the time."

"I think we've got them all, Curt," a man yelled down from overhead. "We picked up the ones at the gate and a man who claims to be piloting the plane outside. There doesn't appear to be anyone else around."

Cheryl saw several people move across the floor of the hangar toward where Curt and Severon had been standing before her fall. She longed to know for herself that all was well with Curt. She tried again to twist around. Just then a hand pressed against her shoulder.

"Relax, Cheryl, you're okay."

It was Curt, and his voice gave her instant assurance that everything would be all right.

He untied her gag and then cut the ropes away from the chair. Helping her to her feet, he assessed her from head to toe. "Are you hurt?"

"No," she managed to say, still tasting the oil on her tongue. "Are you?"

"Nah," he said with a grin. "I'm too tough."

She shook her head, and her legs went out from under her. Curt immediately grabbed her and put a supportive arm around her waist. "Come on. I'll put you in the car until this mess is taken care of."

"I thought he would kill you. He blamed you for Grant, and he said—"

"Don't think about it," Curt replied, hugging her close. "It isn't important now."

He opened his car door for her. "You stay here."

"Curt," she said, taking hold of his arm, "I have to say something."

He gave her such a look of understanding that Cheryl knew no words were necessary. "We can talk later," he said. "Erik and Christy are waiting for us at home, and the sooner I finish up inside, the sooner we can go to them."

"Erik's there?" she said with a voice that betrayed her interest.

"Yes, Erik is there," Curt replied with a grin. "He has something he wants to tell you. Seemed pretty important."

"What was it?" she asked, feeling a surge of anticipation.

"I think I'll leave that to him. You'll just have to be patient for once and do things *my* way."

eighteen

The last conscious thought Erik had was of the clock chiming three times. He fell asleep with his head on the kitchen table, only inches from where his sister dozed. His dreams were nightmares of confusion. He pictured Cheryl in a cage, dangling over a bottomless abyss. He couldn't reach her, and the hopelessness of the situation made him frantic.

At the sound of a car door slamming, he jumped. Unsure if he'd dreamed the noise, he glanced to where Christy had bolted upright. Apparently the sound had been real.

"What time is it?" Christy asked, getting to her feet.

Erik jumped up, his heart pounding fiercely against his chest. He glanced at his watch. "Five-thirty."

They hesitated at the table, their eyes asking the unspoken question of whether they dared look outside. The sound of another car door had them both running for the front door.

Christy beat him and threw the door open with such force that it banged against the wall, breaking the silence of the moment. They moved across the threshold and out on the porch to find Cheryl and Curt coming up the walkway.

Christy let out a shout and rushed down the porch stairs. Cheryl stepped aside as Christy threw herself into her husband's arms. "You're here! You're safe!" She was crying, sobbing, and kissing him all at once. Curt wrapped his arms around her and buried his face in her hair.

Erik held back. Shoving his hands in his jean's pockets,

he exchanged a look with Cheryl that spoke volumes. Curt and Christy moved up the stairs, and as they passed him, Curt leaned toward Erik.

"I told her you had something to say." He winked and went inside the house with his sobbing wife.

Cheryl came up the stairs rather hesitantly. She searched his face as though looking for an answer to some unspoken question. Erik could no longer hold back. He crossed the short space and pulled her into a fierce embrace. For a fleeting moment, he thought she might fight him, but instead she only maneuvered her arms in order to wrap them around his neck.

"I thought I'd lost you," he whispered against her hair.

"I know," she answered softly. "I thought I'd never see you again."

For several minutes they did nothing but hold each other. It was enough, Erik thought. It was enough to know that she was safe and that God had answered all of his prayers.

He pulled away gently and looked down at her. The tightness of her worried expression softened, and she smiled. "Are you really okay?" he asked, fearful of the answer.

"I'm better than that. I. . .well. . ." She glanced away. "There are some things I want to tell you."

"Me, too," Erik said. "There's a porch swing on the east side. Why don't we go sit there and watch the sun come up."

Cheryl nodded her approval and let Erik lead her past the front door and around the side of the stately Victorian home. Erik waited for her to take a seat before joining her. He didn't care what she thought as he put his arm around her shoulders and gave a little tug. Cheryl willingly snuggled down against his shoulder, tucking her head under his chin.

"I love you," he whispered, feeling his heart in his throat. He waited for her to tense, but she didn't. "I think I've loved you for a very long time now." He hoped she'd say something, but she didn't. *Maybe it was too soon*, he thought. *Maybe she will never allow herself to love again.*

"Look," he said softly. "I just wanted you to know how I felt. I know you've gone through a great deal. I guess I just want you to know that when you're ready to love again, I'm here waiting."

Cheryl moved away from him and eased back against the swing. She looked out across the yard before allowing her gaze to rest on his face. "I thought I was going to die," she said simply. "I found myself alone and terrified, and I kept thinking about what you and CJ had told me about God."

Erik grinned. "I wasn't sure you were listening."

Cheryl countered his smile. "I was listening." She grew sober. "I listened just enough to make myself think, and unfortunately at that time, thinking was the last thing I wanted to do. There were already too many things to think about. Grant. My father. The baby. Not to mention everything else related to the last year and a half of my life.

"I wanted to pretend that I could make it all go away. That nothing need ever hurt me again. I wanted to believe that I was alone, because that way I didn't need to worry about feeling anything for anyone."

"But you weren't alone," Erik said softly.

"No, I wasn't. I know that now. I found it out while I was waiting in the back of my kidnappers' van."

Erik shook his head. "What happened?"

"I realized that God really was who you said He was. I wasn't sure how to go about getting Him on my side or putting myself on His side, but I prayed. I really, honestly prayed, and it gave me the courage to go on."

Erik reached out and squeezed her hand. "That's more than I'd ever hoped to hear."

She smiled and nodded her head. "It was more than I'd ever thought possible. I came to realize while I was there, stuck in the middle of nowhere with little hope of escaping, that God was truly there for me. Then I started thinking back to other times in my life when God must have stood by, watching me make my mistakes, knowing that I was too stubborn to be reached any other way. I knew then that He'd been there all along. Even when I was in the pits of despair. Even when I'd made the wrong choices with Grant. God was always there."

Erik quoted the verses from Psalm 139: " 'Where can I go from your Spirit? Where can I flee from your presence? If I go up to the heavens you are there; if I make my bed in the depths, you are there, If I rise on the wings of the dawn, if I settle on the far side of the sea, even there your hand will guide me, your right hand will hold me fast.' "

"Yes," she whispered, and the look she gave him caused his heart to soar. "I tried to flee from God's presence, and believe me, I made my bed in the depths." She lowered her face. "I'm not proud of who I am, Erik."

"But you should be," he said softly. "You're a child of God. Forgiven and purified by the blood Jesus shed on the cross. He took your sins, yours and mine, and sacrificed His life to reconcile us with God. Give Him the past and console yourself in the fact that He blots out your sins and remembers them no more."

"I like that idea," she said, twisting her hands in her lap. "But Erik, the past is hard to forget. There are people who will no doubt help me to remember it on a daily basis."

"Probably. But there are those of us—me for instance—who don't care about the past. We're far more interested in the future and what it might hold in store. The past only entangles us, and Satan uses that to steal away our victory in Christ. The future is our hope in God's ability to take us out of Satan's snares, and the present is where we must act in faith to believe He will do just that."

"And you can forget the past? Forget that I was adulterous with your sister's husband? Forget that I would have borne him an illegitimate child? Can you forget my part in this entire nightmare and still love me? That seems an awful lot to ask."

"But in Christ," he said softly, feeling the pain in her words, "all things are possible, and in Christ, all things are made new. You are a new creation, Cheryl. Why should I condemn you for that which you've thrown off?"

She moved back into his arms and laid her head back until they were cheek to cheek. Together they watched the sky lighten. The colorful fingers of dawn spread out in a blend of lavender, pink, and orange. It was a moment Erik always hoped to remember. A moment that bound them to one another. He would wait forever for her to love him.

Without warning, she got to her feet and looked back at him. "I'm ready," she said softly and extended her hand.

Erik's sense of hope fell hard. He got to his feet and reached into his jean's pocket to retrieve his car keys. She, no doubt, wanted to go home. He pulled the keys out, but to his surprise Cheryl pushed them away and instead reached up to touch his cheek.

"No," she whispered. "I meant that I'm ready to fall in love with you."

Erik couldn't believe his ears. The keys dropped noisily to the porch floor. "You. . .mean it?"

Cheryl nodded, her eyes bright and clear. "I think I've been falling in love with you ever since you showed up at my door with your roguish grin and boyish charms. Facing death made me rethink a few things."

"Like what?" he questioned, gingerly touching her face. He was almost afraid it was an illusion. Her soft skin against his fingers convinced him that it wasn't.

"Things like. . .us. You made me feel whole. You helped me to see hope when I had none. You gave me love when no one else could reach me."

Erik pulled her against him, and with one arm around her waist, he lifted her face to meet his. "I can't believe this is happening."

"Me, neither," she whispered.

He wanted to kiss her. To feel the soft sweetness of her lips against his. He lowered his head to meet her mouth, then hesitated, waiting a moment, as if for permission. Her eyes told him everything. He saw in their blue depths the desire and longing that seemed to mirror his own emotions. Pressing his mouth to hers, he felt her melt against him and sigh. She wrapped her arms around his neck and pressed him closer.

Erik wanted to yell out loud, and when he released her, he did just that.

"I love you, Cheryl Fairchild!" he exclaimed and lifted her into the air to circle round and round with her.

She giggled as he had never heard her do before. There was a definite joy returning to her life, and he thanked God that he could be part of it. He kissed her again.

This time the kiss lingered, and afterward, they simply held each other in the quiet of the morning. Erik felt as though nothing in life could be better. His emotions ran rampant, and his heart seemed to soar on the wings of the dawn. The chains of the past were broken, and now the future could begin.

A Letter To Our Readers

Dear Reader:

In order that we might better contribute to your reading enjoyment, we would appreciate your taking a few minutes to respond to the following questions. When completed, please return to the following:

Rebecca Germany, Managing Editor
Heartsong Presents
P.O. Box 719
Uhrichsville, Ohio 44683

1. Did you enjoy reading *Wings of the Dawn?*
   ❑ Very much. I would like to see more books
      by this author!
   ❑ Moderately
      I would have enjoyed it more if _____

   _____

2. Are you a member of **Heartsong Presents**? ❑Yes ❑No
   If no, where did you purchase this book? _____

   _____

3. What influenced your decision to purchase this
   book? (Check those that apply.)

   ❑ Cover   ❑ Back cover copy

   ❑ Title   ❑ Friends

   ❑ Publicity   ❑ Other_____

4. How would you rate, on a scale from 1 (poor) to 5
   (superior), the cover design? _____

5. On a scale from 1 (poor) to 10 (superior), please rate the following elements.

___Heroine   ___Plot

___Hero   ___Inspirational theme

___Setting   ___Secondary characters

6. What settings would you like to see covered in **Heartsong Presents** books?_____

_____

_____

7. What are some inspirational themes you would like to see treated in future books?_____

_____

_____

8. Would you be interested in reading other **Heartsong Presents** titles? ❑ Yes   ❑ No

9. Please check your age range:
   ❑ Under 18   ❑ 18-24   ❑ 25-34
   ❑ 35-45   ❑ 46-55   ❑ Over 55

10. How many hours per week do you read? _____

Name _____
Occupation _____
Address _____
City_____ State_____ Zip _____

Summer Dreams

*Four all-new inspirational novellas
with all the romance of a summer's day.*

***Summer Breezes* by Veda Boyd Jones**
Law school graduate Melina Howard takes on Blake Allen, a
former sailing instructor, as her crew in a local regatta.

***A la Mode* by Yvonne Lehman**
Small town florist Heather Willis is intrigued when she makes
the acquaintance of a mysterious stranger with a Texan accent.

***King of Hearts* by Tracie J. Peterson**
Elise Jost is a non-traditional student whose life's direction
takes a different course when she makes a high grade with
professor Ian Hunter.

***No Groom for the Wedding* by Kathleen Yapp**
A professional photographer, Penny Blake is capturing her
sister's honeymoon when she finds herself the focus of a fellow
cruise passenger.

(352 pages, Paperbound, 5" x 8")

Heart♥ng

Any 12 Heartsong Presents titles for only $26.95 **

CONTEMPORARY ROMANCE IS CHEAPER BY THE DOZEN!

Buy any assortment of twelve Heartsong Presents titles and save 25% off of the already discounted price of $2.95 each!

**plus $1.00 shipping and handling per order and sales tax where applicable.

HEARTSONG PRESENTS *TITLES AVAILABLE NOW:*

(If ordering from this page, please remember to include it with the order form.)

······· Presents ·······

Great Inspirational Romance at a Great Price!

Heartsong Presents books are inspirational romances in contemporary and historical settings, designed to give you an enjoyable, spirit-lifting reading experience. You can choose wonderfully written titles from some of today's best authors like Veda Boyd Jones, Yvonne Lehman, Tracie J. Peterson, Nancy N. Rue, and many others.

When ordering quantities less than twelve, above titles are $2.95 each.

Hearts♥ng Presents
Love Stories Are Rated G!

That's for godly, gratifying, and of course, great! If you love a thrilling love story, but don't appreciate the sordidness of some popular paperback romances, **Heartsong Presents** is for you. In fact, **Heartsong Presents** is the *only inspirational romance book club*, the only one featuring love stories where Christian faith is the primary ingredient in a marriage relationship.

Sign up today to receive your first set of four, never before published Christian romances. Send no money now; you will receive a bill with the first shipment. You may cancel at any time without obligation, and if you aren't completely satisfied with any selection, you may return the books for an immediate refund.

Imagine. . .four new romances every four weeks—two historical, two contemporary—with men and women like you who long to meet the one God has chosen as the love of their lives. . .all for the low price of $9.97 postpaid.

To join, simply complete the coupon below and mail to the address provided. **Heartsong Presents** romances are rated G for another reason: They'll arrive *Godspeed!*
